To Keep a Promise

By

B.N. Rundell

Print Edition
© Copyright 2016 B.N. Rundell

Wolfpack Publishing
P.O. Box 620427
Las Vegas, NV 89162

ISBN: 978-1-62918-477-7

This labor of love is dedicated to my Sweetheart, Encourager, Editor, and Motivator. I am luck they are all rolled up in the same woman, my wonderful wife. She has chosen to spend most of her life with me and has shown an amazing amount of tolerance, patience and understanding. Only the spouse of a writer can understand the depth of those words and I can honestly say that without her beside me and oft behind me, this would never have become a reality. So, to you, Dreammaker, thanks for the memories!

Chapter One: Discovery

THE DUST STIFLED and choked Jeremiah Thompsett as he struggled to free himself from the makeshift timbers and piles of rock that mercilessly trapped him in the blackness of the collapsed cave. Groping in the dark, he sought relief from the startling pain hammering in his left leg. Despite his efforts, his leg remained immobile under the crushing weight of the debris. He pushed and pulled without benefit of light with every movement magnifying the agony. Jeremiah knew that if he were to be freed, he could not count on help from anyone and he must rely on his own strength and stamina. The last sight of his friend Ezekiel, was the bottom of his moccasins as his bulk disappeared through their cabin door when he dove for cover from the attacking renegades. Ezekiel was a giant of a man whose imposing bulk blocked out the sun with a figure that seemed bigger and blacker than the shadow he cast. His size and basso-profundo voice had earned him the Indian name of Buffalo Thunder. Jeremiah had narrowly escaped into the cavern that the two of them had recently begun to use for storing their pelts and other supplies.

The cabin sat a scant 30 yards from the entrance to the cave that now trapped Jeremiah in its darkness. Since they had discovered this cave, hidden behind tall and thick scrub oak growth, their intentions were to build a better cabin butted up against the opening and use the cave for storage and escape – not as his own prison. Even Ezekiel, for all his size, would have his hands full fending off the marauders that came so unexpectedly into their hidden retreat. Their assault began when they threw the powderhorn charge that brought the loose rock at the entrance tumbling in on Jeremiah. The cave that the two friends were preparing for a refuge, now became a dark and dusty prison.

The thought of Ezekiel outnumbered and in jeopardy brought an even greater urgency to Jeremiah's efforts. Although he knew that Ezekiel was far more capable of handling almost any situation than was Jeremiah, the thought of losing his friend was something that Jeremiah did not want to confront. Now, as his searching had settled on a broken timber, Jeremiah ignored his own pain and wedged the timber beneath what he thought was the largest boulder pinning him down. From his awkward position, he pushed against the dark obstacle with what proved to be a futile effort. With each exertion his lungs filled with the stifling dust and caused a wracking cough that further added to his pain. Feeling his frustration rise, he knew he had to get control and give his predicament the necessary thought. The words of Ezekiel reminded him,

"Boy, no matter what you face, if you take the time to think on it, turn it over in you head, chew on it, and befo' you know it, you gonna whip it. Then ain't nuthin' gonna get the better of you."

Leaning back against the quartz seamed wall, Jeremiah lifted his eyes the blackness that had always tripped the trigger of fear in his mind, and tried to focus on the predicament at hand. He reminded himself, *one problem at a time, don't bite off the whole thing, just this one problem now.* But from the darkness came the questions, *what about the air? Is there enough to last? How can you get out of here?* Although they

2

had used this part of the cavern as a place of cool retreat, he had no idea of its real size. If this was all there was to it, as he suspected, the air would be gone all too soon. And he could not give up hope of reaching Ezekiel before it was too late. Although he had never been known to be defeated in many other conflicts, Ezekiel was badly outnumbered and Jeremiah owed his life to the big escaped slave.

Tight spots were no stranger to Jeremiah. His life was punctuated with those times of narrow escapes and near misses. As he again started digging his leg free, he began to remember.

* * * * *

"JEREMIAH, WE CAN'T LEAVE momma in there, they'll hurt her!"

"Elizabeth, Momma told me to get you and go. Now come on before those Indians figger out that we're missin' and come lookin' for us."

"But Jere . . . "

"No buts, you heard me, now come on!"

With a quick grab on her little arm, Jeremiah had to practically drag his blonde haired sister down the overgrown pathway to the wooded area immediately behind their cabin. It was territory he had explored many times before but then the only dangers were from an overactive imagination of a twelve year old boy. This was different. With fear beginning to pound its own pathway from his heart to his mind and his breath digging its claws into his throat, he thought for a minute that anyone within shouting distance would hear his labored breathing and Elizabeth's whines. That thought just compounded his fear as he stumbled over a log and pulled his sister down with him. Snatching a quick look in the direction of the cabin, he thought he heard a scream from his mother, and with tear-filled eyes, he quickly headed deeper into the woods.

It was a big task for a twelve year old boy. To look after his little sister and hide out from a rampaging party of drunken Potowatami Indians was almost asking too much of Jeremiah. But he had never failed yet and his determination drove him on, trying to keep his tear-filled eyes on the trail with his fingers digging into the arm of his sister. What seemed like hours was only a matter of a few minutes and the two fleeing children found their favorite place of refuge. Where they had before used imaginations to bring forth bigger-than-life adversaries for adventure, they now sought protection from an all too real enemy.

It was late on the second day that Lucas Thompsett entered the familiar clearing that brought the warm feelings of home. With the retreating sun making a slowly fading effort to penetrate the tall Maples with a few shafts of light, the cabin at the far edge now looked serene and peaceful. He anxiously anticipated his favorite moment when his family would spot him and the children would burst the open door with excited greetings and the usual, "What did ya bring us Daddy?" It was that image that he carried with him each time he left on his many supply trips and that same image that hurried his pace home. The picture of his beloved wife, MaryBeth, with her long blonde curls tumbling over her one shoulder and the wrinkles at the corners of her eyes as her smile stretched wide, told of the special bond of love that tied them together. These thoughts hastened his step and his long stride quickly ate the distance to the front door of the cabin. Something was wrong. Dropping to one knee he swiftly brought his rifle up and his eyes searched the familiar scene for the source of his quickly rising fear. The stillness of the clearing betrayed nothing but a single fluttering feather lying a short stride from the step.

As he stepped through the open doorway, the shadowy room was too macabre to be real. It wasn't right. This cabin was *always* tidy, orderly, and clean. What was left of the furniture were splintered pieces in a pile and charred from a fire that had only half consumed the wood. Broken dishes and

4

scattered flour littered the floor. Curtains that had been lovingly sewn and fitted by MaryBeth had been ripped and left in a heap. And blood, blood everywhere. Two long strides took Lucas through the bedroom door to view more mess and disarray. As his stifled scream gave way to guttural groans, he vaulted to the ladder and the loft of his children's beds. It was untouched. His chest ached with the fear that held his breath captive when he first saw blood and now with a scream he burst from the cabin and frantically began his search.

Snatching his rifle from the floor as he ran for the door, he turned to circle the house for some sign. Forgetting the need for caution and driven by panic and anger his first discovery halted him within a few short steps. With tears tumbling down his face and bile filling his throat he tried to make sense of this unfamiliar pile at the rear of the cabin. At the edge of the grisly pile was a ragged bit of the blue gingham dress that MaryBeth wore. Then more as his eyes adjusted to the shadows, the hair in golden curls, a hand that bore the ring of their marriage and had gently stroked his whiskered face, all were now lifeless. He dropped to his knees, choked back his screams and drove his fist into the ground. Then lifting his face to the dark blue of the twilight sky he allowed a cry from deep within . . . "NOOOOOO. . . " its echo muffled in the trees. A one word cry giving vent to his anger, fear, and frustration.

Hearing the familiar voice of his father, Jeremiah stirred his sister Elizabeth to wakefulness. They had hidden in their favorite "hide-out" for a day and a half. It hadn't been easy trying to be brave and to convince her that they were going to be all right. He knew they had to stay here until their father came but they had gotten hunger and Jeremiah was about to try to make it back to the cabin when he thought he heard his father. Their shelter was formed by a mass of roots of the fallen maple tree at the edge of the swampland near the end of their homestead farm. Jeremiah knew this would be one of the first places their father would search for them when he returned from his trip. Many a time the children had played here and their father had helped them make it into a real hideout. He had often told them that if something ever happened they were to stay here and wait for him.

After finding the mutilated body of his wife at the home, Lucas' thoughts immediately turned to his children. *"The kids, where are the kids? Oh, God, please no. Don't let the kids be gone too"* He took to the trail leading to the swampland and their hideout, calling their names as he ran. He stopped, bent over with his hands on his knees, gasping for breath, when he heard the feeble answering voice of Jeremiah.

"Poppa – Poppa – here at our hideout, Poppa!"

Rushing toward the sound of the voice, Lucas saw the children stumbling for him. Dropping to his knees, he caught them in his outstretched arms and sobbed, "Oh, thank God. Thank God you're all right."

* * * * * *

IT WAS A SHORT SIX MONTHS later that Jeremiah and his father stood on the muddy bank of the rushing Kalamazoo River. Aunt Sarah, Lucas' sister, had agreed to take little Elizabeth and raise her with her two girls, it was the best option for everyone. Since the tragedy at the cabin, Lucas had sought some answer for his family. He was lost without MaryBeth and didn't have any idea what to do with a little girl. He loved both his children more than he could even describe but the thought of doing right by his daughter like his MaryBeth would have done, was totally beyond the anything his mind could grasp. Before his sister knew about the attack she had penned her usual letter to her brother and his family and told of all the happenings with her two daughters, school, church and all the joys of family life. Lucas thought the letter was the answer he sought concerning Elizabeth. His return letter to his sister told the sad news and asked for her help, which she immediately offered and now Lucas and Jeremiah turned for a final wave good-bye.

Lucas and Jeremiah had always had a bond with one another and the wilderness and had often talked about a shared dream of the West. Lucas had determined to get as far away from the haunting memory of the grisly scene at the cabin. He wanted to remember MaryBeth as he always pictured her with her golden curls, timid smile, and that special way of standing in the doorway with one hand on her hip and the other waving him home. His only answer was to go, however far in time and miles that it took to let him and his son start over with new places, new dreams and fresh memories. So, together they turned their faces to the West and said, "Let's go!"

The pursuit of their dream had taken the two from the green forested Michigan territory to the gateway of the West known as St. Louis. The ride on the ferry across the Mississippi filled the now thirteen year old Jeremiah with more awe than he thought possible, but that was just the beginning of wonders he was soon to behold. When they stepped on shore and off loaded their horses, Jeremiah turned to his father and said,

"Gosh Pa, I didn't know there was this many people in the whole world!"

Laughing, Lucas responded,

"Well, don't get too caught up in all this activity and doin's, cause just as soon as we get ourselves outfitted, we'll be getting away from here!"

It seemed to Jeremiah that he couldn't move his head fast enough to take it all in, the stevedores on the docks, the paddle wheel steamers coming and going, the people in their fancy clothes mixing with the rough and burley men of the riverfront. The wails of the steam whistles the smells of fish and mud and waste, and the busyness of everyone rushing somewhere and nowhere did nothing but add confusion to Jeremiah's wonder.

"First off, we need to trade these horses for something more suited to the trail. These two were fine for pulling a wagon or a plow, but we need some that will have some bottom to 'em and can carry us the distance we're goin'. Then we'll get the rest of our supplies and hit the trail as soon as we can, it's already gettin' a little too far into summer than I'm comfortable with," explained Lucas to his son.

"What do ya mean, Pa? Is it cuz we need to get wherever we're goin' before snow comes?" queried Jeremiah.

"That's right. Now, let's head up to Choteau road, there's some good places where we can get outfitted. "

Leaning against the top rail of the corral that adjoined the livery, Jeremiah listened while his father dickered with the Livery owner about the trade of horses. Finally settling on a steel dust gelding and a sorrel mare with a strawberry roan mule for packing, the travelers were set to buy and load supplies. Across the street and down a few doors, a general mercantile store promised the needed supplies. Once again, Jeremiah bided his time while his dad negotiated the purchase, and Jeremiah took in the sights from the boardwalk by the hitch rail tethering their new travel partners. Lucas called from the interior of the mercantile, "Boy, come in here and start carrying this stuff out."

As Jeremiah entered with his eyes searching for his father, he noted the grin on his father's face that did little to conceal his father's anticipation. As Lucas leaned against the storekeeper's counter, he cradled a long rifle in his left arm. Jeremiah's eyes widened in youthful wonder as he took in the brass inlay and the maple grain of the stock of the Bedford County Lancaster flintlock long rifle. It was exactly the kind he and his father often talked about. With the buckhorn rear sights with a brass front blade, this was known as one of the most accurate and long-range long rifles of the time. Standing just shy of six feet Jeremiah was just barely taller than this new pride of the Thompsett duo. Lucas held it out to Jeremiah and said, "I thought it about time you had a man-size rifle, boy."

Without a word, Jeremiah lifted the rifle to his shoulder, sighted down the barrel, felt it's balance and knew at once this rifle was made for him. The fit was perfect; the feel of it's browned octagon barrel and the double-set triggers were at once an extension of himself. In .50 caliber, this could bring down almost anything that he could put lead into. Jeremiah was big for his age, rapidly approaching the height of six feet, that of a mature man. It was only his youthful face that revealed his scarcity of years. His frame was beginning to mirror that of his father, broad shouldered, deep chested, with a rugged handsomeness topped off with wavy black hair that was the envy of a raven and now beginning to hide the collar of his homespun shirt. His high cheekbones accented a slightly protruding chin that was common to the English heritage. The family mark of a strong brow spoke of determination and a reserve of strength. Lucas' growing whiskers that previewed a full beard set him apart from the smooth complexioned youthfulness of Jeremiah.

With their supplies snugly strapped down in and over the leather panniers and secured to the wood framed pack saddle, Lucas led out on the steel dust gelding and Jeremiah followed on the sorrel mare while leading the pack-mule. Finally departing the crowds and noise of St. Louis and looking to the trail that would parallel the Missouri River. With little understanding of what lay ahead, their hopes spurred them on. Even before the tragedy, Jeremiah and his father had often wistfully talked of the call to the adventure of exploring those faraway and unknown regions. It was a call that few men really understood, yet it spoke clearly to their souls – filling them with a longing and a challenge to conquer the unknown.

Three weeks of travel did little to dampen their enthusiasm for the adventure, but it did bring a reckoning of the challenges and trials of this new land. With so many days of crossing what Jeremiah was thinking of as endless plains, the foothills finally brought a change to the monotonous horizon. Behind the foothills, the distant blue mountains rose in their majesty to scrape the blue of the clear skies with the granite-grey of their timberless peaks. The Southern end of the Wind River mountain range stretched from North to South and encompassed the entire horizon. Lucas had long dreamed about this time. Since he had first heard and read the first reports from the earliest explorers Lewis and Clark, he knew that one day he had to walk in these mountains. Now, beside the small campfire, it was Jeremiah who remembered his mother and her last words, *"Always trust the Lord, Jeremiah. He'll never let you down."*

But in Jeremiah's simplistic thinking that sprang from a grieving heart, God *had* let him down. His mother was dead, his sister gone, their home burned, and here they were so far from everything he had ever known. Jeremiah thought God probably didn't even know where they were, or for that matter, didn't even care. As he stared into the campfire, the light wisp of smoke twisted its way through the pine needles overhead as the blend of odors mingled themselves with the thoughts and fears of Jeremiah's unusual mix of excitement and uncertainty.

"Son, are you about ready to sink your teeth into this venison?"

As he mustered up a veneer of interest and confidence, he replied, "Sure Poppa, like Grandpa used to say, I'm so hungry my belly button's pinchin' my backbone!"

This was the first deer that Jeremiah had downed with his new rifle and he was proud of his accomplishment. He was beginning to feel like a real mountain man and to be called a real hunter by his father meant a lot to him. And to be able to bring in meat meant he *was* becoming a man. In this country, a boy had to grow up fast and right now a good venison steak would sure help.

Darkness wrapped them in the chilled arms of the approaching fall season. It wasn't the coolness that robbed Jeremiah of sound sleep, but the often recurring dream of his mother screaming for help and his inability to reach her. It had been the same dream since he fled from the cabin and the Indians had so brutally violated his mother. As he tossed on his bed of pine boughs, he wondered if it would ever stop. He knew he couldn't burden his father with it as his father had many nights of tossing and mumbling himself.

10

As the grey light of early dawn awakened his father, Jeremiah was sent down to the creek to try his luck for some fresh trout for breakfast and he willingly sought the relief of busyness. It was probably the lack of sleep the night before that was to blame, but whatever the cause, he dozed off while lying on his belly underneath the willows. He hadn't slept long when the quick tug on his hand-held fish line brought him around. Jeremiah renewed his efforts and a short while later had enough fish for their breakfast. Picking up his rifle, he started back up the hill to their camp under the towering Ponderosa pine at the top of the small knob.

Lucas had taken every opportunity to teach his son the habit of stealth. Whenever they were in the woods, he was taught to watch each step, avoid dead leaves and branches, stones that would roll and cause a misstep and to always be quiet so as not to startle any game they were hunting. Jeremiah now applied all the teaching wanting to show his father how quietly he could move and maybe surprise him on his approach to camp. As he neared the site of their camp, Jeremiah bent behind the scrub oak brush and tried to see through the thick branches to spot where his father would be preparing for breakfast. He couldn't see any movement. The camp was quiet – an empty kind of quiet. The horses and mule were hobbled in the small clearing on the other side of the hill crest and wouldn't be heard, but his father should be moving about. Yet even the slight morning breeze that earlier stirred the pines was still. The grey smoke from the campfire thickly clawed its way upward and obscured the far side of their brief shelter, but his dad would have already taken that down. It was too much smoke; his father always used dead dry wood that would yield little or no smoke.

Feeling uneasy, Jeremiah dropped the stringer of fish as he dropped to one knee and brought up his rifle. He slowly and quietly drew back the hammer to fully set his triggers and be ready for whatever was wrong. He watched and waited, hoping his father would step from behind the trees and call his name asking for his fish for breakfast. Quiet. A sickening smell drifted down the slope and mixed with the sage and cactus but still brought an additional level of caution to Jeremiah. He thought his father could hear his heartbeat as it assaulted his chest and caused his breath to stutter. As he slowly left the concealment of the oak brush he swept the area with suspicious eyes searching for anything that explained the uneasiness. He rose to his full height to see farther up the hill and stepped slowly closer. Looking up the draw to his left he saw nothing alarming, and to his right the hillside dropped away revealing only the meandering stream that turned around the point of rocks and sought the easy way from the mountains.

With each quiet step, fear tried to paralyze Jeremiah, but he fought through the suffocating grip on his heart and mind. Approaching the clearing, the packs and gear that were scattered from the torn shelter began to tell the story that Jeremiah didn't want to hear or see. On the opposite side of the campfire and its thick grey smoke, he spotted what appeared to be a foot. Rushing there without caution, he saw the naked, bloody, mutilated body of his father with the shoulder and left arm still in the fire. Choking down the bile and scream, he grabbed his father's arm to pull him from the fire. Although barely recognizable, the prostrate form was covered with blood and dirt and ash. Most of his hair had burned, but it was still evident that his father had also been scalped and the broken shaft of an arrow protruded from his throat. With his knees in the warm ashes, Jeremiah dropped his head to his father's chest and wept with the choking sobs shaking his body and emptying his spirit of the emotions that had dogged his path for so long.

The stench of burning flesh, dried blood, and ashes of the fire brought Jeremiah back. Rising at the waist, he began to look around and assess his situation. All the usable supplies were gone leaving Jeremiah with only his rifle, possibles bag and the clothes on his back. Looking for some answer to whatever the question was, the only evidence left from the attackers were the many moccasin tracks and one unusual set of boot prints. As his strength began to return, he finally stretched to his full height and stood his rifle against the nearby ponderosa and fighting back the tears, reached down to drag his father's body to the edge of the clearing. Looking down at the bottom of the hill and the stream in the distance, he lifted his eyes to the mountains in the distance with the fresh dusting of early snow. Thinking that his dad would like this place and the scenery, he asked himself, *"Why do people care what the scenery is from a grave? They can't see it anyway."* Then stooping down and using a broken branch from a nearby snag of a dead tree, he began to scrape out a shallow grave. After digging as deep as the rocky soil would allow, he wrapped his father's body in the ragged scraps of their canvas shelter and lowered it without hesitation. Using his hands and occasionally his feet, he quickly covered his father's body. Then picking several large rocks from nearby he covered the gravesite to mark it and protect it from the many varmints in the area.

Now what was he to do?

* * * * *

MOVING THE LAST ROCK that freed his leg brought him back to the present. Drawing his leg free of the rock pile sent a stabbing pain shooting up his leg to his hip and back. Renewing his resolve against the agony, he felt his way to the side of the cave away from the debris. As he leaned against the wall of the cave, he drew a deep breath to fill his lungs with something besides the dust he had been breathing and pushed his back against the cool stone for a brief rest. Leaning his head back to stretch his neck, the perspiration felt cooler on his brow. With his mind whirling, he stretched his neck and head back again. Yes, a slight breeze on his perspiring forehead. That had to mean that fresh air was coming from somewhere.

To Keep a Promise

14

Chapter Two: Finding Daylight

WITH THE MANY TIMES Jeremiah had been in this cave, he now cursed himself for not exploring it any further during those numerous opportunities. But he had never been comfortable in the dark and when the dripping moisture and different noises of water, rocks dropping, and other imagined effects were added, this was not one of his favorite places in which to be confined. But sometimes, you just don't have any choice in the matter, you have to work with what you've got, as his grandfather used to say. *"Yeah, but what have I got?"* he thought to himself. The dust from the entrance collapse still hung in the air making breathing difficult and prompting occasional coughing spells, the rocks strewn on the floor of the cave were obscured by the darkness and caused him to stub his feet and stumble which elicited a fruitless outcry. Frustration began to mount and add to his confusion. Yet, a moment ago, he had felt a draft of air and knew he had to at least find the source.

Stopping and with one hand on the side wall, Jeremiah took a deep breath to still himself and try to focus. It was then the voice of Ezekiel tapped his consciousness, *"Remember boy, when you gits to feelin' fearful, trapped, or such like. Stop.*

*Then look 'round wit yo mind and yo eyes and then look agin
and consider it all, very careful like. Den let all yo senses tell
you what yo need and listen. Den, you can find a way."* He
knew he had to stop and let those words work in his mind and
his senses, all of them, have their way.   Still favoring his
injured leg, Jeremiah now made himself very still, to listen,
feel, taste. There, on his face, that smell – that was *fresh* air.
Carefully moving toward the source, he had to slowly though
blindly feel his way. Bracing himself against the sidewalls, he
stumbled further into the cavern. His breathing was a little
easier away from the dust of the entrance, but every step
reminded him of his injury. Hand over hand feeling his way
in the darkness – the shuffling of his moccasins whispering
through the empty cavern.

Feeling a splash of cold water at his feet, Jeremiah dropped
his hand to discover he was at the edge of what seemed to be a
small pool of water. The dripping on his shoulder revealed the
source to be seepage from above. Considering his position
carefully, he pictured the terrain outside the cavern. Since the
mouth of the cavern was high on the shoulder of the hill behind
the cabin, the interior had to drop down and go under the small
stream that ran into the clearing North of the cabin. But how
far did it go? And where was the source of the air?

Now on his hands and knees, bypassing the pool, Jeremiah
made his way deeper into the cavern. Trying again to stand,
the low and uneven ceiling forced him back to his knees. The
space was gradually getting smaller but the air continued to
filter through its distant opening. The pain in his leg caused
him to drop to his stomach just as a sudden flurry swept over
his head – bats! But they came from behind him, that meant
they were going to another opening! He had managed to
continue his struggle by focusing all his senses on every effort
to make his way and was determined to make it out. But his
injury, waning stamina, and rising frustration were combining
to bring discouragement. He never thought something as
repulsive as bats would ever be an encouragement to him, but

that is exactly what he now felt. Now, with his strength returning, Jeremiah pulled harder in the direction of the flight but came up short as his head thudded against the rocky end of the grotto. With a muttered "ouch" he grabbed his head with both hands and rolled on his back. It was only the quickly recalled memory of his mother and the bold-eyed look she would give him, that kept the stream of curses from pouring forth. Opening his eyes to what he expected would be more darkness, he was surprised to see a small glimmer of light far above him.

Dropping his hands from his head and focusing his eyes on the light above, Jeremiah was able to make out a chimney-like opening stretching nearly 30 feet overhead. 'Maybe this is my way outa here,' he thought as he squirmed himself upright in the narrow cleft. *"This is gonna take some doin' now, I don't mind tellin' ya,"* he muttered to himself. The challenge was to get his bulk through an opening that didn't pose any problem for the bats. The rock surface was smooth and free of any apparent handhold. Desperate not to be disappointed, Jeremiah began to wedge himself upwards. The small shaft of light presented hope that renewed his determination and gave strength to his will.

He had no way of knowing the forces that shaped this chimney-like opening, but he was thankful it was there. The smooth rock surface was a continuous cliff side feature that might have been a crevice widened by weather or water, but whatever forces shaped it, it was devoid of any protrusion that would be a handhold. The stone was predominately deep red with vein like streaks of lighter shades and even browns and tans. He thought it might be sandstone, but was too hard and smooth. *'So, how do I get up there?'* Leaning against the left side, he turned his back to the wall to enable him to look up. Putting one foot on the opposite wall to relieve the weight on his leg and hip, he pushed himself back. Then, he thought, *'Maybe if I push . . . '* and with that he lifted himself off the floor and was suspended with the pressure of his back and his

17

foot. Then, using his back and upper arms, he began to inch his way upwards. With mostly upper body strength and pushing his feet against the opposite side, he made more progress. The farther he climbed, the wider the opening – which gave him more light, fresher air, but the far wall was now almost too far to get good pressure. Pausing to consider his next move, the opening was now in sight yet still out of reach. And would it be big enough? Jeremiah filled his lungs with fresh air, but it was tainted with the taste of smoke.

* * * * *

AFTER EZEKIEL HAD TAKEN the slug in his right chest, he turned to make it to the cabin. Pursued by the renegades that were now riding hard after him and screaming their curses while firing their pistols, the big black man disappeared into the doorway. He didn't know how many there were nor why they were after him, but he had spotted at least three on horseback before he hit the doorway. Now Ezekiel cracked the shutter on the one window to provide a firing slot and moved the muzzle of his long rifle up to take a shot at a fleeing renegade. These weren't Indians, these were white men! The hammer fell; the pan opened, ignited the powder and fired the charge in the barrel. White smoke belched from the muzzle as the .54 caliber ball sought its mark between the shoulder blades of the buckskin covered would-be assassin. With his spine severed the man fell on his face and did not move. But the others had found cover behind the large copse of spruce. Ezekiel rolled away from the opening to grab his possibles pouch and powder horn to quickly reload his rifle. Taking stock of what was happening, he sought an answer to why they were here. Surely it was a mistake, or they thought he had something of value like pelts or gold or something. That had to be it. The mountains were often a hide-out for those that were too lazy to work and make their own way through life and chose instead to take it from others. No matter where you were, there was always some form of evil, or so his Momma used to tell him.

Maybe they were slave catchers? No, not here. But his musing was interrupted by the thunk of arrows hitting the logs by the window opening. Then he smelled the smoke as the logs began to ignite.

* * * * *

WHEN JEREMIAH FILLED his lungs with the fresh air and smelled the smoke, it didn't set easy as he was reminded of the ongoing battle between Ezekiel and the band of renegades. After all Ezekiel had been through, surely this wouldn't be enough to do him in. Of course, Jeremiah knew that many good fighters could be taken down with a lucky shot – it only took one.

Just above his head he saw a cleft that was big enough to get his hand into. If it went to the top of the opening, maybe, just maybe he could stretch up and push with both legs and reach it. With a deep breath, he tensed the muscles in his legs to push up as he reached overhead for the crevice. The sudden searing pain shot through his leg to his back and he recoiled in pain. Jeremiah lost his footing and scraped his back on the rough surface of the sidewall as he plunged downward. Grabbing for handholds that weren't there, he continued to fall and was stopped only as his body wedged itself painfully in the narrow chimney. Slowly letting his breath out, Jeremiah mentally checked himself for further injuries. Other than some bad scrapes on his back, arms, and legs, he seemed to be all right. Without the durable buckskins, his injuries would have been much worse. No broken bones, his one leg still very painful, and the added pain from his fall, he slowly began retracing his route to the top.

By placing his hand in the crevice and making a fist, he was able to pull himself to the overhead opening. The hole that admitted the light and air might have been a good escape hatch for the bats, but it needed enlarging to allow Jeremiah's bulk through. The smooth rock surface formed a slight shoulder which made a shelf large enough for him to rest upon. Again drawing deep breaths of the fresh air, Jeremiah began his examination of the opening and evaluated his situation. The light and air streaming through the small portal were exhilarating but also taunted him in his predicament. Reaching to the opening, Jeremiah felt around the edges and cracks, and feeling the loose gravel and sand, he realized the blockage was not an impenetrable obstacle. A sizable boulder partially obscured his escape and was held in place only by its weight on the gravel beneath it. Jeremiah began to twist around to shift his weight on the small shelf and place his back against the boulder. Wedging his good leg in the crevice that had been his handhold, his other foot with a toehold on the edge, and knowing his leg would complain in pain, he began to push against the boulder. Every muscle in his legs bulged and rippled and he tried to find a handhold to give extra leverage, but the boulder didn't budge. Filling his lungs with the smoke tainted air, grimacing with his face, gritting his teeth as if the facial muscles would make the difference, he dug deep into his pool of desperation and pushed again. The only result was a few small pebbles of gravel and grains of sand falling down his escape shaft and bouncing below.

As the sweat dripped from his brow and trickled down his face, he tasted the salt, licked his lips, drew another deep breath and sought to draw from any reserve strength deep in his bowels, and pushed.

"You can do it boy – come on now, don't let ol' Ezekiel down – I knows you got it in you!"

The encouragement from the past was all he needed to make good his escape. The rock rolled clear and was replaced by the blue sky of freedom. Jeremiah's grin covered his dirt and sweat stained face as he pulled himself in the welcome daylight. Rolling over on his back and staring to the beautiful blue of the overarching sky, he took a brief respite to enjoy all that was before him.

Before standing, he rolled to his stomach to survey the hillside that fell away below him. Realizing he was now on the backside of the hill that shadowed the cabin, he noted the timber that spread its skirt of deep green on the shoulder below and wound its way around to the Southern face that sheltered the cabin. Still favoring his bad leg, he began to climb to the crest of the small scrub covered knob. Upon approaching the crest, he bent at the waist and continued up ensuring he did not expose himself. Knowing a skyline reveal was easily spotted, he dropped to his knees and went the last few feet on hands and knees. As he thought, he was on the North side of Fiddler Creek and a short distance from the cabin.

Jeremiah slid away from the crest and made his way to the edge of the timber, knowing the trees covered the shoulder of the hill and provided good protection between him and where he wanted to be. He breathed deeply then stealthily made his way with the pine needles quieting his approach. His leg slowed him down considerably but he soon cleared the creek and was nearing the back side of the cabin when he again smelled smoke, a lot of smoke. Knowing the need for caution, he again stepped cautiously forward, feeling the softness of the forest floor through his soft soled moccasins. Steadying himself with a hand on the nearby towering Ponderosa pine, he felt the roughness of the bark and the sticky pine sap that lent a bitterness to the fragrance of the pines. But with the bittersweet smell of the pines, the throat scratching smoke, the mud of the nearby creek, another stench from his past again assaulted his nostrils, burning flesh.

He was certain the renegades had torched the cabin, and if it burned, what about Ezekiel? Now down on his belly, Jeremiah slid through the grass that in the shadows still held the dew of the morning and the dampness permeated his buckskins while the fear filled him with an unfamiliar aching pain. The monster of a black man had been his friend, father,

21

teacher, and even protector for most of the years of his youth and early manhood. The thought of anything happening to him, spurred Jeremiah onward.

Reaching the edge of the clearing, he surveyed the entire area for any sign of the chaos that had invaded their sanctuary. There were no renegades, horses, nor Ezekiel. With the smoke hanging low like a morning fog, Jeremiah stood amid what was now a totally unfamiliar sight. The grass of the clearing had been torn and ripped by the marauders horses scrambling in the melee. The cabin that had stood as a sentinel over the glade, was now blackened log ends and ashes that bore mute testimony to the battle that had been waged. The clearing was unusually quiet. No screech of an overhead hawk, no croak of a magpie nor the argument from a camp robbing jay, no chirping squirrels nor groan from the timber, all were quiet. It seemed to Jeremiah that even the nearby stream had been hushed as the stench of death hung heavy in the glade.

Now certain he was alone, Jeremiah stepped toward the cabin's remains. Afraid of what he would find, but knowing what awaited him, he began to pick through the burnt shell with little hope. The largest piece of roof timber was partially covered with a sizable square of sod. Pushing the grass covered sod aside with his mocassined foot, he spotted the partially burned beaded medicine pouch staring up at him and telling him what he didn't want to acknowledge. Now filled with rage and anger and almost blinded by tears, he grabbed the timber and cast it aside as if it were a mere twig. The blackened, partially fire consumed body of his friend was revealed. Lifting his fist to the sky and facing the white tufted blue mantle of the heavens, Jeremiah let loose a guttural cry.

"AAIIIEEEEEYAW . . . WHY . . . WHY do you always take them from me? What did I ever do to you!!"

As the frustration overwhelmed him, he stooped in anger to free the body of his friend. The stench of burned flesh mingled with the breath robbing smell of ashes, as he dragged the blackened buckskins encasing the lifeless form to the rear of the cabin site. It was at the foot of the tallest pine that Ezekiel, known to his adopted Arapaho family as "Buffalo Thunder" would rest. This is where the two of them had made their plans to free Ezekiel's family still held as slaves in the Kentucky territory. It seemed incongruous that here in this place where those dreams were voiced, that those same dreams would come to such an unexpected end. But that was the way of life and death. The time between the two is measured only by memories made, promises kept and plans made and realized. Promises kept – as the promise made between these two blood bound friends. A promise to free those that still longed to taste that elusive delight called freedom. A promise whose heart gripping memory now made Jeremiah realize that the mantle of responsibility had now fallen on his shoulders. To keep that promise meant he must do all he can to deliver Ezekiel's family from slavery!

After burying his friend, Jeremiah scattered burned timbers and ashes to obscure the burial site. Some tribal practices encouraged warriors to ravage gravesites of enemies to mutilate the bodies causing the dead man's spirit to wander defenselessly on the other side. Although neither of them followed the beliefs of the Plains Indians, there was something unsettling about that thought. As he pulled himself erect, Jeremiah's body complained about its treatment by sending stabbing pain through his leg, side and shoulders. The tattered buckskins did little to hide the matted blood and dirt from his injuries incurred in the cavern. Hunger pangs reminded him he hadn't eaten since late yesterday. The whispering breeze slipped through the pines and brought the beginning of night in its skirts. The accompanying coolness brought the realization to Jeremiah that he was unprotected from dropping temperatures. This did, however, tend to remind him that he was alive while his friend lay in the new grave. He didn't know what to say, he didn't have any flowery words like the preacher said over his mother's grave, so he simply turned his face upward. As the trace of the earlier anger began to surface, he

23

said, "Alright God, you wanted him so bad you couldn't wait. I guess he's in your hands now. He used to say he looked forward to seeing you, I don't know why, but I figger if what he believed was true, he's there with you. Let him have it pretty easy, if you don't mind, cuz he shore never had much of a break down here."

Jeremiah's eyes lingered on the rising full moon for only a moment before his inner senses prompted him to seek shelter. As he made his way into the copse of pines, the pale yellow moonlight danced around the shadows to point the way. Stooping under the low hanging branches of the tall Ponderosa, he dropped to his knees to prepare his bed. Hollowing out an area in the long pine needles, he burrowed into the concave bed site. Scooping armloads of needles over his legs and then his torso, he let exhaustion take him captive and dropped into the abyss of sleep.

Chapter Three: Changes

THE THIN SLIVER of orange that marked the Eastern horizon began to push away the gray of early morning as Jeremiah rustled his sore and stiff body from his bed of pine needles. The dimly lit clearing before him brought the memory of yesterday's horrors to storm into his consciousness. Where once had stood the cabin that had been a place of learning and refuge for Jeremiah, only a few scattered stones and stubs of logs remained. An unlikely due, Ezekiel, the giant of a black man who had become Jeremiah's replacement father, and young Jeremiah, the misplaced orphaned youth, had spent many special days in and around that cabin.

More than any other place, to Jeremiah, this was home. Although the years of his youth and early adulthood had been split between here and the nomadic Arapaho camps, this was the only place that offered any permanence, any security, and now all that it had previously offered, was gone. As he indulged his memories, his eyes lingered on each reminder of special times and deeds. A tree with a blaze they used for a target, the big flat boulder used as a workbench, the cluster of aspen that marked their cache of trade goods and supplies, the kinnikinnick bushes by the trail to Fiddler Creek and their diggin's. Their diggin's – the gold! They had made several trips to what Ezekiel had called their "glory hole" at the fork in the stream and with several months of labor had accumulated 18 pouches of gold in both dust and nuggets this year alone before the hole was exhausted. Each pouch easily held 15 to 25 ounces of almost pure gold. The gold was to buy the freedom for Ezekiel's family, his mother, two brothers, and one sister still held as slaves on a plantation in Kentucky. And now, if that was gone, there would be no way he could keep his promise.

Jeremiah ran to the cabin's remains and vaulted the ruins to the corner that marked the place where the parfleche with the leather pouches was kept. Again throwing aside the remaining pieces of burned wood, the revealed indentation in the ground told Jeremiah what he feared. Somehow, the renegades had found and taken the parfleche. To Ezekiel the gold had been the price of freedom for his family and maybe even to clear his own name. Jeremiah again looked to the glade and then to the grove of aspen that marked their summer's cache. At least it was undisturbed. That meant the previous year's take was safe, but he would also need to get the stolen gold back if he expected to keep the promise to Ezekiel and free his family.

The plan for freedom had been formulated over the years of Jeremiah's growth to manhood. Ezekiel knew an escaped slave could never return with any amount of gold and live long enough to free anyone. Many times he had said,

"Yassuh Jermiah, just like God sent dat prophet of old to set his people free, God done sent you to me to hep set my fambly free."

In August of 1831, in Virginia, a slave named Nat Turner had instigated a slave rebellion that resulted in 57 white people dying and over 100 slaves losing their lives by the angered whites. The word had spread throughout the South and made its way to the Kentucky plantation where Ezekiel labored. Ezekiel's momma had told him that Nat Turner was her nephew, the only son of her only sister, and she begged Ezekiel not to listen as the many other slaves were clamoring for him to lead a similar rebellion. Although Ezekiel was primarily a house slave and a companion to the owner's son and had gained a second-hand education in the many ways of the whites, the overall slave population looked to him as a leader. As he yielded to his mother's wishes, his heart longed for freedom. He believed his only chance was to escape and then seek a way to free his family with a plan formulated from the bastion of his own freedom.

It was this long ago nurtured idea that evolved into a plan. Upon arrival in Kentucky, Jeremiah was to play the part of an aristocrat type and Ezekiel as a gentleman's gentleman. By pretending to be a land speculator and developer, Jeremiah would have need of experienced workers and would seek to buy them from area plantations as needed. It would take considerable formulating and even more money to accomplish, but the reward of seeing his family free would be worth the risk. Now it would be up to Jeremiah, not only to regain the stolen gold, but to find Ezekiel's family and gain their freedom.

The sun had burned away the morning mist as Jeremiah turned his back to the memory-laden grove and started on the trail to the Arapaho encampment. He didn't look forward to telling Ezekiel's Indian family. Walking Dove was Ezekiel's wife of 6 years and the mother of his five year old twin boys, Chipmunk and Badger. Jeremiah knew he needn't concern himself with her future as her family would assume the responsibility to take care of them. The boys' uncle, Spotted Elk, would become their father figure. Elk was a respected member of the war council and would be certain that his sister and nephews would be well provided for and protected. Jeremiah sympathized with the boys, well understanding what they would be going through in the loss of their father. Among the *Baasawuune'na* or Brush Hut tribe of the Arapaho, Buffalo Thunder, as Ezekiel was known, was considered one of the tribe's greatest warriors and it was an honor to be a part of his family.

Jeremiah still favored his injured leg as he began his trek to the summer site of the village. The trail he followed rose to the upper reaches of the pines that stretched to the timberline of the rock strewn mountain. It was not an easy climb on foot, but the horses had been stolen by the renegades and the trail usually taken on horseback was longer though easier. Jeremiah opted for the shorter distance, knowing he could make it even though hindered. But since his injury was more muscular bruising and sprain, he felt the trail was not insurmountable.

As he reached the upper heights, the timber changed from the lodgepole pine and spruce to the windy pines that yielded to the cold winds of the higher elevation. With branches like arms stretching to the lee side of the wind and the trunk facing the wind embarrassed by the cold and turning red, the trees pointed the way downward to the valley that held the village. But their strange appearance also warned Jeremiah of the impending cold winter winds that awaited only the call of old man winter before they unleashed their icicle laden wrath on any unprotected traveler. The continual teaching of Ezekiel had taken root in Jeremiah's mind and now reminded him to focus on his objective without being distracted by pain or obstacles. The trail now dropped to the lower reaches of the forest and the vegetation gave way to smaller pinion and oak bushes. His buckskins were tattered and didn't provide much warmth or protection from the "wait-a-bit" thorns that reached out to hinder his slow progress on the dimly marked trail. Forcing his way through the brush, he stepped into the first small clearing that revealed the tall Wind River mountain range that rose with outstretched granite arms and cradled the valley below. He could smell the coming storm. In the high country it was easy to see the threatening snow in the distance as it obscured the tops of the granite peaks. Jeremiah knew he would have to travel through the night to make it to the village before he was caught by the early season storm.

By nightfall, he had cleared the timber and started across the large park that was dotted by the moonlit shadows of sagebrush. Picking his way carefully, Jeremiah sought to avoid being too visible in the dim yellow glow of the now vigilant full moon. Although in Arapaho country, it was not unusual for raiding parties from the Shoshone or even the distant Crow tribes. There was always some young bucks looking for the honor of leading a successful raid on the hated enemies of their tribe. Horses and scalps were the most sought after prizes, with the horses used for trade and status. A well used trail crossed the meadow a short distance ahead. The pale light would soon be hidden in the rapidly moving clouds that were now winning the race with Jeremiah. He had little reason to be concerned this close to the village, but danger stalked the unwary and unprepared. At the intersection of the trails, his eyes followed the wider well-worn trail Northward and easily detected the signs of recent travel. Without better light it would be impossible to learn who and how many had passed this way, but the obvious presence of shod hoofprints told him this was also the trail of the renegades.

The thought of the murderers of Ezekiel rekindled the fires of anger in Jeremiah and threatened to overwhelm him. His first impulse was to turn and follow the trail, but his reason and resolve gave rise to his well-ingrained discipline and he instead quickened his pace to the village. This was not going to be a quick hunt and to go without provisions and preparation would only insure his failure. Now was the time to focus his energy toward this more immediate goal.

"What'eer you do, boy, don't go bitin' off more'n you can chew. Ease up on it, take it one step a'time and there ain't no problem gonna be able to git ya down."

His father's voice from the past intensified his resolve. This hunt was going to be unlike any other he had ever undertaken. Never before had so much been at stake and never before had he been so alone.

The first light flurry of snow was the early "dry" type with big fluffy flakes that drifted slowly down through the pines and did little to hinder his progress. He had made it across the park-like meadow and was now in the thicker pines that surrounded the low shoulders of the foothills. He knew this trail and could easily traverse it under any condition. As was his habit, while almost mindless traveling, he began to formulate his plan of action and calculate his needed supplies.

"I'll need enough supplies for two or more weeks, that means two horses. My other set of buckskins, two new pairs of winter moccasins – Walking Dove makes the best and she'll gladly make them. My medicine parfleche. Maybe she'll let me have Ezekiel's spare long rifle and skinning knife," he pondered.

Jeremiah and Ezekiel had planned on returning to the camp before the tribe moved to the Southern foothills for the winter and had already laid in some of their winter supplies so stocking up for the trip should not be a difficult task. He had plenty of robes and pemmican and other essential supplies in his hut. The thought of his warm capote and a bowl of Dove's elk stew brought a smile to his face. He thought of his close friends Broken Shield and his sister Laughing Waters, they too would be saddened at the news he bore. When Jeremiah had first arrived at the village in the company of Ezekiel, he hated all Indians. Potowatomie Indians had slaughtered his mother, Shoshone dog soldiers had mutilated his father, and the thought of any Indians being anything but monsters was a thought he didn't entertain.

But the patience and discipline of Buffalo Thunder had slowly opened his mind to the realization that people were what they were not by the color of their skin, the clothes they wore, the place where they lived, but by the character within their spirit and the life that revealed what their heart held deep within. There were good and bad among any group of people,

30

no matter the color, language or land. The recent raid had certainly revealed the evil that resided even in his fellow whites. His mother had often tried to get her family to accept each person on their own merits. The Arapaho were an open people, willingly giving to and learning from all who crossed their path. Broken Shield and laughing Waters were leaders among the young people and eagerly accepted Jeremiah when they saw he would not be daunted by the usual childhood games.

They had been friends since Jeremiah first proved himself as a "warrior in training" with the rest of the young people in the camp. In every contest, Broken Shield and Jeremiah were always the best, usually alternating winners. The best, that is, until Laughing Waters had bested them both with her skill with a bow. The skill came from a combination of her extraordinary craftsmanship that built her bow, laminated with red willow, cherry, and spruce woods, and the way the bow seemed to be an extension of her spirit. Because of this and other skills, she was considering the path of a warrior, an unusual move for a woman but not unaccepted. Broken Shield and Jeremiah, or White Wolf, his warrior name, had proven themselves in the sun dance and become warriors. But for a woman to take this path required a decision of the council and Laughing Waters had not yet decided. The thought that the three had been inseparable friends undoubtedly weighed on her decision. Many had thought that White Wolf and Laughing Waters would become mates but the two of them never showed each other anything more that their deep friendship. There had been times that White Wolf had thought Laughing Waters as a possible mate but such thoughts were replaced by more urgent matters of becoming a warrior.

Cresting the ridge that overlooked the tree lined meadow that held the encampment in its embrace, Jeremiah knew the wolves, those warriors that were always on roving guard, had already sent word to the village that he was coming. He never tired of the scene of serenity of the peaceful village below.

31

Although known as the Brush Hut tribe, many of the families had adopted the hide covered conical frame known as a tipi as used by other plains tribes. Referred to as lodges, these made up most of the dwellings with the remainder being dome shaped brush hut lodges. All the lodges had their doorways facing the rising sun in the East. The *Hinanea'ina* or the People, as they referred to themselves, were peaceful and very family centered, caring deeply for one another and especially their children.

Jeremiah allowed himself the luxury of a few moments to drink in the scene below him. Seated in front of a few lodges were the ever-present old and wise men with their all-purpose birdwing fans. Leaning against the willow backrests, their complacent appearance belied their watchfulness, and though with an aged look to their wrinkled bodies and snow capped brows, their very presence lent an air of security to the village. Several children were noisily playing the hoop game just outside the circle of lodges. Drying racks held fresh strips of meat while chattering women gathered together to scrape the new hides and gossip about the toils of life and the budding romances among the young people. By the lodge of Night-killer, a young warrior, a circle of men had gathered to make a new supply of arrows, one shaping flint points while others stripped and painted shafts and still others fitted feather fletches. It was a typical day in camp, full of joy and expectation and hope.

As Jeremiah expected, he could see the shadowy outline of both his friends standing in waiting outside Shield's lodge.

"Ya ta hey nähaba'hää, my brother. Your return is sooner than expected and you are alone," said Broken Shield, stating the obvious.

"Greetings to you Broken Shield and to you Laughing Waters. Yes, I am alone but with a heavy heart. My *neisa'na,* my father Buffalo Thunder has crossed over to the other side and is now with Manitou."

Their usual stoic faces now registered surprise as images of the great warrior Buffalo Thunder danced across their memories. Through the years and many battles, Buffalo Thunder had made himself known as a great warrior. Because of his prowess and leadership, the tribe accepted him into their fold and he soon proved himself capable of a position on the council. This had never happened before, for anyone to even be considered for such an honor, he must show himself without enemies and greatly respected among their ranks. His reputation soon spread to the other tribes and he quickly gained the respect of all that knew him. Even the enemies of the Arapaho held his reputation in high regard. Because of his many victories and honors in battle and even in friendly competition, the possibility of his death had not even been contemplated.

"Come into my lodge and share your heart, my brother. Tell us of your father." Shield had spoken to Jeremiah, but also motioned to other nearby council members and leaders.

As they stepped through the flap covered entryway, the many aromas so common to the lodges of the people brought the warm sense of home to his mind. The wood smoke from the cooking fires, the sage used for cleaning and purifying the lodge, the many smells of foods, and the pleasant scents of buckskin and buffalo robes all wrapped themselves around Jeremiah and lent the sense, though temporary, of security to Jeremiah. It was the lodge of Shield's family, his father Tall Lance and his mother Red Deer. The father was seated on robes opposite the entry and his mother already busied herself fixing a stew for the visitors. As the group seated themselves cross-legged around the fire pit, Jeremiah began to relate the events of the preceding days.

To Keep a Promise

Chapter Four: Companions

AS THE NIGHT LIFTED its canopy of darkness to reveal the first muted rays of sunrise, signs of life were plentiful in the village of the Brush Hut tribe. The array of lodges and huts of the encampment all faced the light of morning as it made its debut in the East. While the tops of the pines that formed the village backdrop were being tipped with the pale pink from the paintbrush dipped in the sunrise, several tendrils of smoke from the cooking pits snaked their way heavenward.

Jeremiah made his way to the lodge of Walking Dove to tell her of their loss of Ezekiel. She was a large woman and stood half a head taller than any other woman in the tribe. Before Ezekiel came, her size had intimidated any possible suitors. Although strikingly beautiful she feared she would never have a mate. Jeremiah knew of the practice of the plains Indians to show their grief by some form of self-mutilation and he had prepared himself for her response. As he began to speak of the battle with the renegades and of Ezekiel's death, her wail of grief began a slow ascent from deep within until it escaped with such force that it startled him. As Dove fell to the floor of her lodge, she groped through her tears for her fleshing blade. Before he could stop her, she made three quick slashes on her left arm and blood began to mingle with her tears.

Her wails of sorrow brought other family and women from nearby lodges. Making their way into Dove's lodge, the women gently pushed Jeremiah to the entrance. This was a time for those that had suffered similar loss to give comfort. The men had to deal with their grief in other ways – vengeance or battle. But this time was for the wife of the slain warrior, Buffalo Thunder. She would grieve, but she would want a part of the vengeance, either by participating or by helping those that would go on this vengeance quest.

Broken Shield stepped beside Jeremiah as he exited the lodge of Dove.

"Walk with me my brother," he said as Jeremiah pulled himself to his full height.

With long strides, the two friends made their way to the edge of the village to the slight rise overlooking the meadow. The horses from the encampment were lazily taking their fill of the dew covered grasses watched over by the young men basking in the morning sun at the edge of the glade. The two figures presented an impressive appearance as they stood together. Shield wore his hair in the tradition of his people, parted on each side, while in the middle, over the forehead, it was left standing upright. A zig-zag edge marked the hairline over the temples, while the rest of his hair hung loose over his bare shoulders.

Jeremiah, now in new buckskins, contrasted with Shield with his black hair hanging loosely to his shoulders. Jeremiah's darkly tanned features resembled the natural coloring of Shield. Both standing just over six feet, their stance reflected the blend of confidence and grace evident in both men. Shield's sharply chiseled features contrasted with Jeremiah's rugged handsomeness, although there was enough similarity that they could easily pass for brothers.

"We will go with you," Shield flatly stated as they sat on the large boulder.

Jeremiah was not surprised by his friend's statement. He would have done the same thing if the situation were reversed. Jeremiah dropped his eyes to the bright orange flowers struggling through the stones at his feet and let his mind work the possibilities of his response. The task fell upon Jeremiah as the adopted son of Ezekiel. The vengeance quest was the burden and privilege of the sons first, then the brothers or the father and uncles. Ezekiel's twin sons were too young and with no other family it became Jeremiah's responsibility to avenge this warrior's death.

"This is not your battle," Jeremiah responded.

"We are brothers, we have always been together. We will be together in this also."

"I can't ask you do that, Shield. You're needed here with your family, for the move to the Winter dwelling place."

"This is something that must be done and we must do this together. You may think you are a great warrior, but I know you and there are too many for one man." Shield's resolve, apparent in his expression, did little to hide the humor betrayed by the wrinkles forming at the corner of his mouth.

"The council must decide this because of Thunder's standing as a member," reminded Shield.

Jeremiah had not considered the council although he knew Shield was right. He had been driven by his anger and need for vengeance and was only concerned about beginning his pursuit as quickly as possible, for he knew the renegade's trail would not be easily followed after too long a delay.

"All right, Shield. You tell the council I'll meet with them as they request. Only try to encourage them to do it quickly. The early snows are against me and I must be leaving."

"It is good."

As they made their way back to the encampment, Jeremiah again reviewed his list of supplies he would need and the preparations that must be made for his departure. He wanted to travel as light and fast as possible, but most importantly he must be well armed. He knew Walking Dove had some of

Ezekiel's trade rifles and she would be willing to stock him with powder and shot. A good bow was also necessary and the best bow maker was Black Kettle, the village medicine man, and Laughing Waters father. Jeremiah turned toward the lodge of Black Kettle, slapping Shield on the shoulder as they separated.

Nearing the lodge of Black Kettle, he called out the customary greeting expecting to hear the voice of the old medicine man in answer. Instead it was the familiar voice of Laughing Waters that called out.

"Enter White Wolf, you are welcome in our lodge."

Pushing the flap aside, Jeremiah entered the warm and inviting lodge of his childhood friends. The well-banked fire glowed warm from the central firepit. Cooking stones were carefully arranged to absorb the heat in preparation of the coming mealtime. Hanging from the lodgepoles was an assortment of drying roots, leaves and other unidentified shriveled items. He recognized several drying clumps from his time of study with Black Kettle. He easily identified niibaatou (hemlock-leaves), biihtceihina (a yellow composita), niäätä (a greasy carrot-like root), and niox (sweet-grass). Kettle had hoped that White Wolf would decide to follow the medicine ways and be groomed to take his place but the council resisted approving an adopted nih'aca (white man).

Seating himself against the willow backrest, he turned to Laughing Waters, and was again entranced by her beauty. Her dark hair lightly reflected the glow of the fire as the straight length gently fell over her shoulders. The white soft tanned buckskin dress and matching moccasins and leggings accented the womanly curves and contours that revealed her lithe figure. Although this attire was more often worn for special occasions and ceremonies, Jeremiah sensed this time was somehow special to Waters. Her aquiline nose was highlighted by the deep pools of mystery in her eyes. Slightly parted full lips were pursed in the playful pout and frown so familiar to Jeremiah. But the familiar girl warrior appearance had been replaced by this image of womanliness. He knew no other woman whose beauty stirred the attentions of every man in the village, both young and old.

"What are you doin' in the lodge at this time of day? Shouldn't you be out practicing with your bow so you could learn to hit something with that thing? It seems a shame that you waste that fine piece of workmanship you and your father made."

His attempt at humor betrayed his feelings of uncertainty at this new image of Waters and his slight smile did little to hide his envy of both her skill and the laminated red willow bow, for her expert marksmanship was well known. None in the village could compare to her ability with this weapon of warriors.

"Practice is only necessary when you are learning, which is something you've yet to do."

Waters tossed this remark over her shoulder at the idle man in her lodge.

"If I had a bow like that, I wouldn't need to practice either," he answered.

That friendly banter came from years of practice and continued until Black Kettle entered the lodge moments later.

"Ahh, White Wolf, it is good to see you. But my heart is heavy with the news of your father's passing to the other side," stated the gray haired medicine man as he seated himself.

"As is mine, Black Kettle. But my sorrow is tempered with the need for vengeance against those that have done this thing. I must soon leave."

Black Kettle bent forward to reach behind the leather parfleche and boxes at the rear of the lodge to retrieve his latest creation. With pride, he lifted the strong red willow longbow and extended it toward White Wolf.

"The spirits made this one especially strong. Only a great warrior will be able to draw an arrow with this bow. An old man like me no longer has the strength. Take it my son, and may the great Manitou guide your arrows."

As his fingers lightly grasped the gift, Jeremiah's eyes practically glowed with admiration for the craftsmanship of the master. The hand grip had five smooth layers of sinew and the red willow was laminated with cedar for strength, all tightly bonded together with thin layers of smooth sinew. It seemed to have a life of its own and easily became a natural extension of the arm that held it.

"This is a great gift. I am not worthy of one so fine, Uncle," using the term of respect.

"It would honor me if this gift would honor the memory of your father," spoke the respected statesman.

With a stolen glance at Laughing Waters, Jeremiah said, "I will carry this with pride and the memory of its maker will make its use always honorable."

Laughing Waters followed Jeremiah from the lodge. Once outside, she said, "I will join you and Shield on this quest."

"You cannot. This may be a long and very difficult journey and we don't know where it's going to take us. I can't ask you to do this."

"You didn't ask me, and you can't stop me. You need someone along that knows how to use one of those," she stated with a casual motion toward his new bow as the smile tugged at the corners of her mouth.

Jeremiah knew little about women, but Ezekiel had taught him enough to know it is useless to argue with one so determined. He never won any debates with her before and he knew it would be fruitless to attempt to do so now. Shrugging his shoulders in a sign of surrender, he swallowed his feelings of frustration and impatience and stepped off to find Broken Shield and learn of the council's decision. He had been prepared to meet with the council but he also knew that it would be unusual for them to summon him, he would not be needed for them to make the decision that Jeremiah knew would come.

Tethered by the lodge of Walking Dove were two well-groomed horses. One was a dark chestnut with a smattering of white on its rump, a blaze face accenting the fire in his eyes. Standing just over 15 hands, the stud was well muscled and built for stamina.   Jeremiah recognized it as the favorite hunting horse of Buffalo Thunder, known for its strength and speed and envied by everyone in the camp. Usually the favorite horse would be killed and left at the grave of its owner, but Walking Dove did not choose to sacrifice this fine animal. Another of his many favorites would be taken to the grave.

The other was a buckskin with a well trimmed black mane and tail. Although smaller than the appaloosa, it had been bred for strength and endurance. Two better mounts could not be found. The buckskin was packed with several rawhide bags and parfleches stuffed with all needed supplies for his quest. Jeremiah knew there would be venison jerky, pemmican, dried camas root, and a good variety of other edibles, as well as blankets and robes for the coming winter. He recognized his own medicine parfleche and his possibles bag among them. Dove exited the lodge holding a beaded and fringed rifle scabbard with a burled walnut and brass mounted stock protruding. Extending it toward Jeremiah, Dove said,

"Ezekiel was saving it to give to you on your next birthday."

Gently drawing it from the soft leather scabbard, Jeremiah beheld the remarkably fine crafted .54 caliber flintlock. The dark grain of the stock emphasized the brass mounting that accented the handiwork, with a cap at the fore end of the stock that secured the wiping stick, a patch box blended in the scroll work of the brass on the opposite side of the cheek rest, and the heavier brass that fit the butt of the stock for the muscled shoulder of the marksman. Lifting it to his shoulder and sighting through the buckhorn sights, he marveled at the balance and sense of strength it elicited. The rifle fit him as if it had been built just with him in mind. Trying the lock and double set triggers, he knew this was an exceptional rifle and his heart swelled with the memory and thoughtfulness of both Ezekiel and Dove. The words of Ezekiel came to mind,

"A weapon should be the extension of a man, add to his strength and confidence. It has to be a part of you, not a burden to you."

Although the words of Ezekiel, the expression was not characteristic of him. It was the time spent as the companion of the plantation owner's son and their conversations that brought such eloquence of thought.

Dove told Jeremiah, "Remember as you go that Buffalo Thunder will be with you. And as you seek his murderers, think of his woman, the pain in her heart and the emptiness in her lodge."

Dropping the butt of the new rifle to rest on his foot, and lowering his voice from the enthusiasm and excitement he felt, he responded, "My heart is also empty, and I feel anger but it is not anger that drives me. I made a promise to Ezekiel to free his other family, his mother and brothers and sister. To do this, I must retrieve the gold stolen by the men that murdered him. If vengeance comes, it will be because the spirits will it."

Broken Shield had silently approached behind Jeremiah and now said, "It is good that anger does not push you. Anger can affect your judgment and your reactions. You must always be in control of your feelings and do what you must to complete your quest."

Shield was leading his pinto hunting pony loaded with his weapons and supplies.

"I see the council agreed with you," stated Jeremiah as he turned to face Broken Shield. The two grasped forearms, their eyes revealing their anticipation of the coming journey. Jeremiah looked over Shield's shoulder to see Laughing Waters approaching astride her sorrel mare that always pranced with quick steps anticipating a hunt. The mare lifted its stocking feet high betraying that eagerness that all felt. Now the three childhood warriors in training were to begin this quest of warriors. They had often been together on hunting trips, but none had been involved in a quest such as this. Each one knew that the coming days held the unknown.

Chapter Five: The Pack

LIKE A SILVERY SNAKE, the small stream worked its way through overhanging willows that occasionally drooped their branches into the water as thirsty vagabonds looking for relief. The stream seemed out of place in the dry rock strewn and sagebrush bearing shoulder of a valley that hung from the side of the pinion covered foothill. Bordered by a cluster of spruce and pine with a sprinkling of stray aspen, the entire valley was dwarfed by the towering crags of granite that stretched to the blue of the sunlit sky. From the hill strewn horizon in the North to the flat plains horizon in the South, not a cloud revealed itself in this panorama.

But the peacefulness and beauty of the area was marred by the mixed band of six horsemen, four white men and three Indians, that cautiously rode across the open meadow, with heavy brow shadowed eyes seeking any sign of danger. Guilt does that to a man. When that knowledge of wrongdoing weighs upon a soul, he will judge everyone and everything from the perspective of impending judgment. He will always be trying to justify his own actions by condemning others and excusing himself, ever trying to escape the consequences of evil deeds. Obscured from their view were the smaller

43

foothills separating them from their goal of Two Bears pass that knifed its way through the imposing barrier of granite. An odd mixture in size, shape and temperament, the seven men were bonded more of necessity than purpose.

They were in the land of the Hinanae'ina, the feared Arapaho that were known for their fierceness in battle. Few were the tribes that compared with their skill and bravery in battle. Although future generations of the Arapaho would be at peace with the white man while others continued to war, now the Arapaho were to be feared, for they were not known for their kindness to intruders into their land. The caravan of renegades was anxious to be gone from this area and away from the constant threat of wandering hunting parties and certain and dangerous conflict.

As the hooves of the horses whispered through the grasses, the gravelly voice of the one known as Hawg broke the somber mood as he asked, "Frenchy, ya think that injun'll find anythin' up thar?"

Lucuque DuBois, known as Frenchy, was the unkempt but undisputed leader of the bunch. A smaller than average man, his single distinguishing trait was the meanness and hatred that always glared from under his massive black eyebrows. Sagging jowls and whiskered face did little to cover his mottled skin or hide the deep black of his eyes. Conscious of his build that lacked anything resembling shoulders, he always wore his Hudson Bay blanket capote, thinking the bulk of the coat gave the misimpression of size. In any physical contest he would be the loser except his willingness to kill without conscience either by his hide-away pistol or his skill with the razor sharp knife would change the outcome in his favor. The fear instilled in his followers was never to be perceived as respect and now with a battered beaver top hat, another attempt to increase his size, he sat astride his tall bay gelding.

At midday, he had sent one of the three Indians in their group to scout the trail to the pass and to find a spot to camp.

44

With the usual attitude of irritation in his voice, he now responded to Hawg's inquiry.

"What difference does it make? Ya worried about sompin' Hawg?"

"Aw, Frenchy, you know I ain't worried. Just wonderin' that's all. I just don't like the idear of meetin' up with a bunch o' them 'rap-hos. I could handle three or four, but I'd git tired after that."

"Don't worry 'bout it, Hawg. You're too big and ugly for any of them to mess with you."

"Ya think so, Frenchy. Ya really think they won't mess with me? Huh?"

Without responding, Frenchy hung his head and muttered in his turned up collar. The big man's real name was Alonzo Hays but his nickname fit better. A massive man of almost 300 pounds, his long legs hung below the belly of his horse and often dragged in the tall grass. What he lacked in intelligence was made up for in strength. Frenchy first met him after seeing the big man kill a mule with one blow to the side of its head. When asked why he did it, the response was, "He was on my foot and wouldn't move. So I moved him." That action ended his job of plowing the farmer's field and Frenchy offered to let him tag along with him.

The conversation had drawn a third man to move to the front of the column. With a slight build, stringy hair that would be blond if ever washed that now protruded from under a ragged floppy and pinned back hat, Emity Chase, known simply as Kid, sounded off. "I hope we do run into a bunch of them 'Raphos. I'd like to send a few of them to foller that nigger we sent to glory!" As he spoke, he jerked his Ketland flintlock belt pistol from beneath his oversized black coat and took aim at an imaginary foe.

The spring fed stream that coursed its way from beneath the stand of willows at the edge of the meadow stopped the procession as the horses dropped their heads for the long awaited drink. The first to slide from his horse was the last of the white men, Almon Rosencrantz. He plopped his pot belly on the small strip of sand and buried his face in the cold stream. Up current from the horses, he placed his hands on the sandbar and lifted his upper body free of the chilling wetness. The blood from the wound in his upper arm colored the water as he had continued to bleed from the wound received the day before. But this did not hamper his thirst. With a quick shake of his head, he freed the remaining water from his VanDyke style moustache and beard, while a few drops coursed over his large jowls. It was all he could do to push himself up on all fours and struggle to get his one leg up to slowly rise. While many men of his size were surprisingly strong, Almon was nothing but very fat and awkward. His presence was a mystery to all but Frenchy and Almon didn't hesitate to let everyone know how much he detested being away from real civilization.

Without warning, Frenchy pulled on the lead rope of the pack horse and dug his heels into the ribs of his mount and started through the small stream, stirring the rocks and silt to muddy the water. The others quickly mounted to follow, fearful of being caught without cover and alone. The two Indians allowed their horses to satiate their thirst and each stooped and scooped water in their hands to satisfy their need. The smaller of the two, Horse Catcher, rode a skinny sorrel mare that lunged up the slight dirt bank. Grabbing a handful of mane, he laid himself along the top of the mare's neck to give his little weight to her efforts. As his horse caught its footing and then stopped near the willows, the sun silhouetted Horse Catcher and revealed his thinning hair and a receding hairline that accented his wrinkled forehead. A single feather tenuously clung to the lock of hair draping over his shoulder.

With a look of disgust, Yellow Cloud, broad shouldered, tapered torso, and muscular arms that made up his imposing figure, nonchalantly walked his long-striding pinto across the water and easily stepped up the opposite bank. Showing his characteristic distinguished look of disinterest, he shook his single scalplock at the crown of his head and casting a glance from his deep-set black eyes, he kneed his horse to follow the pack of white men.

Frenchy led the pack horse and column into the trees that bordered the meadow. The diminishing light caused each rider to dip his head as if enabling his eyes to penetrate the receding darkness. There was always light in the forest, but it filtered through the higher branches of the needle covered pine and upon reaching the forest floor was distorted and blended with the varying shades of shadows. The tight grouping of tall Ponderosa to the right of the trail cast a long and dark shadow over the trail where a fallen tree blocked any progress. Frenchy's tall bay had dropped his head and shifted slightly to the left without any warning. The snap of a stick and the creak of the wind driven snag deeper in the forest spooked the bay. With his head now dropped between his front legs, the bay side-hopped and quickly kicked his rear feet as high as possible, letting his rider know this horse wanted to be gone from this place. Trying to unseat his rider over his head, he again kicked his rear feet high and arched his back. Unsuccessful, the bay jumped back as if his front legs were mounted on springs. Sucking his lungs full of air, the horse put all his efforts into ridding himself of his rider. Launching himself as his hind feet kicked loose from the ground covered pine needles, and sent careening through the trees and dark shadows accompanied by the screams of the man that gripped the saddle horn with both hands. The darkness obscured the rotting timber that now flipped horse and rider head over heels.

The deep pine needles and other forest debris cushioned the fall of Frenchy, but even though he suffered nothing but bruises, his pride was crushed and anger kindled. He shakily pulled himself up beside the tall pine. Then in a fit of anger, he pulled his knife from his boot scabbard and ran to the still form of the horse and began to repeatedly plunge the knife into its neck and shoulders. With each stroke, he screamed and grunted, venting his anger. The blood splattered over his arms and chest and face making his fearful figure even more intimidating.

Sensing a presence behind him, he spun around to face his previously dispatched scout, Walks-in-Water, now seated solemnly on the rotting log that had upset Frenchy and his horse. Without reaction to the crimson soaked madman, the Indian said,

"The horse can only die once. It is foolish to try to kill that which is already dead."

He stood and turned to go to his ground-tied horse in the shadows.

"We make camp ahead."

With his mouth agape and gasping for breath, Frenchy watched as the renegade Arapaho warrior rode away toward the trail now obscured in the shadows. Frenchy then stooped and pulled his rifle from its scabbard, checked it for damage, picked up his battered top-hat, and started to follow Walks-in-Water. As he neared the trail he spotted Hawg standing next to his horse and holding the lead rope of the pack horse.

"Don't just stand there, Hawg. Get back over there and get my gear out from under that dumb horse, gwan' now." He motioned with his loosely held rifle in the direction of the carcass to emphasize his command to the big man. Without hesitation, Hawg dropped the lead rope and stepped out to get the gear as ordered. He soon returned with saddle and packs draped over his shoulder.

Frenchy had dropped the pack from the gray pack horse and now reached for his gear to prepare to saddle the gelding. He tightened the cinch on the saddle, slid his rifle in the scabbard, tied his bedroll and other gear on behind, then mounted to leave.

"Uh, Frenchy, what about the pack here," Hawg asked, motioning toward the pile on the ground at his feet.

"You carry it – you're as strong as any horse." Without looking at the exasperated Hawg, Frenchy kicked his horse to move up the trail. He still had madness and meanness coursing through him at what he perceived was the stupidity of his big bay and refused to admit to himself that he was also at fault for rushing into the shadows. This was typical of the Frenchman. From his boyhood, he had refused any responsibility for what he did and usually sought to blame anyone nearby to escape his consequence. As is true of those that are devoid of real character, Lucuque DuBois had been scorned by anyone that came to know him and his real nature. The only company that tolerated his bankruptcy of integrity were those that were likewise equipped with little more than greed and selfishness. This like-mindedness of all in this crowd made their association understandable, for each one thought the practice of using others or taking from others to accomplish his own ends made him smarter than those that gained their goals by hard work or their own resources.

Frenchy arrived at the campsite where Almon, Kid, and the three Indians had already begun to arrange their packs and start a fire. The camp was well situated, just off the trail with enough tree cover at the edge of the clearing to filter any smoke from the campfire and make the camp less conspicuous. Frenchy's expression stifled any remarks as he dropped from his horse to establish a claim on his choice for his bedroll. Throwing his gear in a heap at the foot of a large pine, he turned with a scowl to face the others whose conversation and action had suspended upon his arrival.

"Whatsamatta with you?" He yelled at the circle by the beginnings of a fire.

The shout stirred them to action as each one looked away from Frenchy and busied himself with whatever caught their attention. Frenchy had led his horse to the picket line, secured him, and returned to prepare his bedroll. Hawg walked into the campsite, the large packs hanging from his shoulders, then led his horse to the picket line. He cheerfully greeted the camp and began to secure the gear. Without noticing Frenchy's demeanor, he asked, "You think them 'Rap-hos care about what we did to that big black man?"

"Now why would a bunch of dumb Indians care about some ole' slave?" replied Frenchy, irritation still showing on his face.

Walks-in-Water spoke up, "The big black man known as Buffalo Thunder was respected among his adopted people, the Bääsawuune'na. When they find him, they will seek vengeance."

"Well, we got a plenty big start on 'em. With that other'n dead in the cave, it'll be quite a while 'fore anyone knows what happened. By then, we'll be long gone from here," responded Frenchy.

The tension in the group seemed to lessen with Frenchy's answer. The memory of the long ride without a meal stop brought the attention of the group back to practical matters. The readying of the meal was done by Almon and the Kid while the rest prepared their bedrolls. Without any more conversation, the men drifted into individual thought of the future days and the journey ahead.

Chapter Six: Journey

THE SUN HAD REACHED its zenith in the azure blue that stretched itself over the jagged peaks

that still held their recent dusting from the early winter storm. As the trio passed the fringes of

the encampment of the Brush Hut tribe of Arapaho people, the lone wolf on the ridge

overlooking the camp lifted his feathered lance in salute. Many of the other young warriors had

wanted to join them, seeking an opportunity to try their skills against the enemy and bring honor to their tribe. The council had consented to Broken Shield and Laughing Waters only after Shield had petitioned them of the need for Buffalo Thunder to be avenged. No other warriors would be risked.

The mounts were as eager as the young warriors who rode them. With a steady though somewhat fast pace, the quest had begun. Mid-afternoon brought them to the meadow where Jeremiah previously spotted what he thought was the trail of the renegades. Shield's skill at tracking made him invaluable to the small group. Although Jeremiah was better than most, Shield had proven the better of the two. Shield dismounted and casually walked through the tall grass, hands and eyes moving back and forth across the trail for sign. Dropping to one knee, his hand lightly brushed aside a few leaves to reveal a patch of dirt with clear hoof prints. Shield stood and turned to join his friends as they stood silently beside their horses, patiently waiting as the mounts gained their fill of water from the small stream.

"Seven or eight, all mounted or packed heavy, not in any hurry. They're headed NorthEast, maybe to go through Two Bears pass. About two days ahead."

"Then let's hit the trail, we still have 'bout four hours of daylight," responded Jeremiah.

The winter storm that Jeremiah had anticipated the day before had passed over leaving little more than a trace of snow in its wake. This high up in the mountains, early snows seldom lasted more than a few hours as the bright sun quickly melted it away. The sky above them was an azure blue without a trace of a cloud, but the Westerly breeze carried the threat of still another storm. Confident in Shield's leading the way, Jeremiah allowed his mind to reflect on the previous days events. The memory of the burned remains of his friend that was an image seared into his mind and gave rise to previously quelled emotions. Knowing that anger and grief both work to distort a man's judgment, he worked to methodically sift through his feelings and come to grips with the problems at hand.

The tug on the lead rope from the pack horse turned him around and his eyes settled on Laughing Waters. A slight smile touched her mouth as her eyes caught his and held them in a lingering gaze. She had a way of making him uncomfortable that he didn't understand. He valued her friendship and was begrudgingly pleased that she had insisted on coming along. Somehow a grief shared, even in silence, is the easier borne. He didn't know if he was challenged, encouraged, or threatened by her confidence and skill as a warrior, but he was pleased that she was with him and not against him. She would certainly be a formidable enemy.

The trail ahead now held his attention. They had entered the stand of pines that bordered the meadow-like park and would soon be on the rocky trail to the summit of Two Bears pass. The passage was silent, with the horses hooves made quiet by the pine needle covered path through the forest. The mountain-bred horses readily picked their way around the fallen tree covering the trail. The only noise the occasional creak of protest of a weathered snag rubbing against the bark of another tree. As the trail entered a narrow clearing, Jeremiah noticed a ponderosa pine that stretched high above them, with a bark splitting trunk the size of two large men, it bore the deeply imbedded and yellow territorial claw marks that stretched as high as he could reach standing in his stirrups. Nodding toward the marks, he said,

"That's a mighty big bear, and those are fresh too." His remarks were just loud enough for Waters to hear and she responded, "You better hope he's turned in for the winter. We don't need to be looking over our shoulder for some grizzly wanting to fatten up before he sleeps."

"Ah now, surely you aren't afraid of a lil' ole' griz' now are ya? Just think what a pretty necklace his claws would make around that delicate neck of yours."

"That's just it. The only way I want them around my neck is on a string, not while they're still attached to that tree topper."

The trail bent around a shale-strewn shoulder to reveal a wide smooth knob. Shield had dismounted and was on one knee examining the tracks ahead. As he felt their presence, he spoke over his shoulder, "There are seven horses – there is one missing. It entered the woods but didn't come out. That might be what the bear was upset about. One carries a heavy load, a big man. His feet hang below the horse's belly and rub the dew from the brush. Another one still bleeds. The one that leads is nervous and jittery and is on a small mount with short strides, but quick. They passed here in the morning, two days ago."

"That's them," said Jeremiah, " . . . seven of them. The sign around the cabin showed the same except for the wounded one. I thought there were more, but if there were they left a different way and I never found any other sign. At least Ezekiel drew blood before they overwhelmed him. I didn't get a good look at any of them when they attacked. Just before the blast at the cave, I did see one on a small dapple-grey horse and another on a tall bay. Maybe he was the leader. All I remember was a funny lookin' black hat."

Laughing Waters nudged her horse forward and spoke to Shield, "You and White Wolf go on ahead and find some shelter for camp. I'll look around for some fresh meat and catch up." Without waiting for a response, she dropped off the trail into the trees and brush beside the stream. With an understanding born of years together, the two men turned to follow the trail into the mountains. They came to a large rock slide area and dropped down to lead the horses across the unstable shale stone. The experienced horses were a wonder to watch as they cautiously picked their way across, testing each step before trusting. Their light steps reminded Jeremiah of an old grandma tip toeing through her favorite flower garden. Spring water broke through the rocks at the edge of the slide and cascaded over the trail, pooling in one of the few level spots. There was no reason to stop as they were well supplied and fresh water was abundant on this side of the pass. They were on the Southwest side of the mountain, entering a cut between two peaks that towered well over timberline, as the sun dropped from sight and slowly began to paint its exit with the brilliant shades of orange and gold.

The trail entered a grove of aspen still clinging to their leaves of gold though rattling them like stuttering troublemakers in the early evening breeze. It was familiarity that turned Shield behind the large boulder to a shallow cave with a large overhang. This was a shelter used by many before them and was well kept. The overhang was black with the smoke of many previous cookfires and the circle of stone marked the common firepit. They could safely build their cookfire without the glow being seen farther than a few feet from the boulder. No one would detect their presence.

The clatter of hooves on stones warned of Water's return. She had known of this shelter from earlier hunting trips when they had ventured to the high mountains for the sweet meat and white pelts of the mountain goats. Sliding from her mount, she casually dropped three snowshoe rabbits by the firepit. "Do you think you two mighty warriors can do anything useful with those?"

With a grin at Broken Shield, Jeremiah said, "Well, I can skin 'em for you, but beyond that I think it takes a woman's touch. Don't you agree, Shield?"

"All my father taught me was to bring it home, then it was up to the women," he replied with laughter in his voice. Their easy banter continued until after they had eaten and were ready to roll up in their robes for the night. With the horses staked by the boulder, their vigilance would make rest easier for the trio.

The well rested mounts stepped to the trail with an eagerness and quick pace which put the travelers nearing the crest of Two Bears pass by full daylight. Wanting to gain time on the trail of the renegades, their early morning meal of pemmican and water was taken while traveling. The fresh snow of the storm that whistled by them in the night, was enough to cover the trail and obscure any fresh sign. Now relying on instinct and their proven ability to think one step ahead of their adversary, they approached the most perilous part of the mountain pass. The steep and narrow trail switched back and forth over loose rock and grass covered tundra to gain the altitude of the crest.

As Jeremiah led the winding column, he watched a marmot duck behind the larger of several boulders beside the trail. Jeremiah's eyes continued their roving quest for sign, any sign. The marmot dislodged a rock that tumbled beside the trail, the spot was dark red and out of place. Blood. With one still bleeding, the renegades would be forced to either stop and tend him, or leave him behind. Either way, it would help to slow them down, giving a slight advantage to Jeremiah and his friends. Every sense and intuition told Jeremiah this was going to be a long and tenuous hunt.

Chapter Seven: Grizzly

THE ROCKY ESCARPMENT rose as an over towering sentinel above the travelers as they topped the trail on Two Bears pass. The trail continued on a Northwesterly course, but dropping to the lee side of the dominant wind, the trio sought a brief respite and a time to blow for their mounts. On the crest behind them, the windy pines held their ceaseless vigil with their blushing faces turned windward and their outstretched limbs behind them. Jeremiah remembered the first time he saw these strange trees with branches on only one side. He and Ezekiel were scouting for new trapping country and their journey took them into the high country in the spring of his 15th year. When he had asked the seasoned mountain man about these strange trees, Ezekiel replied, *"Just look at yerself. You be standin' thar wid yer back to de wind and yer arms flappin' in de breeze. An' iffen you was to stay dat way, yer backside would be as red as dem trees too!"*

The loss was still fresh and like a wound that tries to heal and it is picked at, it continued to bleed. Many times every day Jeremiah was reminded of his friend and each thought brought clenched jaws, squinted eyes, and thoughts of vengeance. Pushing himself on, he urged his appaloosa below the crest of the pass and on the trail. Dropping below timerline, the hunter's view of the trail ahead was now obscured by the tops of the fir trees sheltered on the leeward side of the mountain.

Still in the lead, Jeremiah sought to maintain their pace and quickly led the trio down the trail leading into the dark timber. He knew that if they were to find any sign of their adversary it would be where the trail had been sheltered from the previous night's storm. It had been two years since he had traveled this trail with Ezekiel, but his memory was clear. As with most high country dwellers of that era, landmarks, trails, mountains, streams, and even stories told form a mountain man's atlas that can be readily called upon as needed. When the two had gone to the only rendezvous Ezekiel attended, Jeremiah was amazed as he listened to the mountain men share tales and stories complete with vivid descriptions of the trails and country they traveled. It seemed to the youngster that nothing ever slipped from the memories of these early explorers.

Now remembering an aspen filled draw with a spring fed stream, Jeremiah resolved to stop for a short rest and a meal. The slight breeze slipped through the shadows and rattled the leaves of the aspen and stirred the growing whiskers on Jeremiah's face. The stubble was short but he knew a beard would give needed protection from the high country's wintry winds, and also add maturity to his still boyish face.

The early afternoon's sun filtered its rays through the tops of the taller fir and then crowned the tops of the aspen, then stretched its rays of warmth to the grass carpet of their nooning spot. Waters had put the rest of the rabbit on sharpened willow branches and hung it over the small fire, the horses grazed on the nearby grass and Shield and Jeremiah had stretched out on the sunny spot. It was in quiet moments like this that Jeremiah found himself turning introspective. *"What is my life going to be like now? The only life I've known has been with Ezekiel and my Indian friends. How am I going to be able to keep the promise to Ezekiel? What was it he always said? 'Jus' take*

*one day at a time, boy. Da Lawd goes wid us ever' step o' da
way. He ain't neber gon' leave us.'"*

Back on the trail, the stutter step of his appaloosa brought
Jeremiah back to the present. The horse was skittish and his
attention was focused to the right near the edge of the trees
where the draw fed its stream to the meadow. A large growth
of kinnikinnick hindered Jeremiah's view of the open meadow.
His horse's ears were pointed forward betraying its fears while
its breath was drawing deep and fast. The buckskin packhorse
now pulled against his lead rope and stepped quickly to the side
of the trail distracting Jeremiah and threatening the precarious
balance of his rifle now nestled in the crook of his arm. A
quick glance behind him revealed Shield and Waters pulling a
tight lead on their horses as well. Each of the riders tightened
their grip as they bent low and spoke quietly and calmly to
reassure their mounts.

With a deep seat and chest hugging legs, Jeremiah pressed
his heels to his horse's ribs, leaned over his neck with the reins
loose to encourage his mounts movement, he now cautiously
led the group to the edge of the clearing. With wide eyes in
the direction of the horses' continued concern Jeremiah sought
to stay in the shadows of the trees. Not certain of the cause of
alarm, he noted a stretch of fallen timber at the border of the
meadow. Thinking only of potential enemies, Jeremiah was
scanning the clearing and timber for any sign of impending
attack. And then he smelled it – and a mountain of brown
exploded from the bushes to the right. The angry bellow that
belched from the cavernous mouth of the towering grizzly sent
horses and riders scattering.

With a scream, Jeremiah's appaloosa sidestepped so fast
and far, Jeremiah thought he was suspended in mid-air, but the
stud's confusion and fear brought him back under the now
scrambling rider. Jeremiah clawed for the saddle and sought
to pull himself back up, then the buckskin jerked free from his
startled grip and fell backwards with his back feet curled under
him, his head yanking right and the mane flying left, eyes

bulging and his teeth grabbing nothing but air. The slipping packs now pulled the buckskin down and with one step and a careening swipe of a massive paw with claws 5 inches long, the grizzly laid open the neck of the pack horse, exposing its now useless windpipe.

The noise uttering from the throats of the terrified horses could only be described as a scream, screams that added to the terror and panic felt by every living being involved. The massive roar of the grizzly, now standing to his full height of at least 12 feet, drew the attention of all and further added to the fear at the sight of the massive mouth and teeth that snapped and dripped with drool and the blood of the packhorse. Waving his arms for his balance, he seemed to claw at the very existence of all creation that dared to be in his presence.

The bedlam increased as Shield's mount, with his head low, mane flying, and tail signaling his exit, galloped for the black timber with Shield gripping reins and mane to keep from being scraped from his back. Waters' crazed mount clawed at the sky as it reared high to unseat its rider, toppled over backwards and pinned Waters underneath.

Jeremiah dismounted, whether by his intent or with the help of the bucking horse that catapulted him, he was on his feet with his rifle in hand and flung the fringed sheath from his weapon. Before he could take aim, the bear dropped to all fours and headed for the now trapped Laughing Waters held helplessly beneath her struggling horse. With renewed effort, the horse lunged to its feet to make its escape. The unconscious woman now became the intended victim as the bear lumbered ever nearer. Bringing the .54 to his shoulder, Jeremiah quickly drew a bead as the bear reached Waters' still form. The hammer dropped to the frizzen, sparks, the whisper of the flash powder and the reassuring blast from the muzzle seemed to take an eternity, yet the ball found its mark behind the small ear on the massive skull of the silver tipped grizzly. In mid-stride the brown bulk dropped as if it had been pole-axed, its head landing atop Waters' legs.

Dropping his rifle and pulling his Green River knife from his belt-scabbard, Jeremiah bounded to Waters, prepared to finish the battle with the bruin. His efforts were needless as the bear was unmoving in death. Grabbing one fore paw, Jeremiah struggled to roll the monster from Waters still form. Lifting her to his chest, he carried her to a carpet of fallen pine needles beneath a towering ponderosa. As he brushed the dirt and needles from her forehead, she began to stir to consciousness.

As her eyes met his, she saw the look of more than brotherly concern and her heart was stirred with her oft felt longings to be held by this man who kept himself so distant, so alone. As the memory of the bear returned, her compassionate look was replaced by one of fear as she quickly sat up and searched for an answer to her confusion. Seeing the prostrate form of the bear, she looked at Jeremiah with a question in her eyes. To the unspoken question, Jeremiah responded, "It's all right now. That ole' grizz ain't havin' us or anythin' else for lunch today."

She continued to search the small glade for sign and asked, "Where's Shield, and where are the horses?"

"Well, I reckon it'll be a while before Shield gets that horse of his to slow down and turn around. But when he does get back here, then we'll go lookin' for the others. I 'spect they'll slow down when they get winded and can't smell ole' bruin here. The question is, how are you?"

As she quickly scanned herself and probed her mind for indications of pain, she replied, "All right, I . . . think." Flexing her arms and legs she stretched to rise from her hastily made bed in the shade. "Everything seems to be working."

The afternoon shadows had begun their stretch to meet the coming darkness when Shield returned with both Jeremiah's appaloosa and Waters' sorrel mare in tow. None of the mounts appeared to be injured, but the dried lather showed the chase to be a long and tiring one. The trio would have to make camp where they were to give the horses a chance to rest. Waters and Jeremiah had already moved their gear from the fallen pack horse a good distance downwind from the carcass of the bear, knowing the horses would still be skittish. Laughing Waters had skewered bear steaks cooking over the small fire as the men staked out the horses in the tall grass at the edge of the clearing.

"My brother did well – it is not easy to kill a bear such as that one," said Shield as he motioned to the claws now drying on the sun-soaked fallen log.

"Well, for a bit there, I wasn't too sure but what that woulda been our bones dryin' in the sun."

"This will make for fine telling at the story fires when we return. Our brother White Wolf will be known as the great bear slayer," said a somber Shield.

Grinning, Jeremiah replied, "And is everybody goin' to know what a great horse racer Broken Shield has become? I mean, after all, the way you high-tailed it outta here when that bear tried to lay out the welcome mat, a man would think you weren't friendly at all, Shield."

Chapter Eight: Ambush

THE DARK CLOUDS at the Western horizon hinted at an early dusk and the rising of another winter storm. The diminishing light drew the pack from the deeper darkness of the trees as they sought a protected but readily accessible campsite for the night. The break in the trees was on the Northeast slope and still high enough to overlook the disappearing trail that led to the Clark's Fork of what would later be called the Yellowstone River. With a sudden stop, the horse's hooves rattled the stones in the trail and brought the riders attention to the leader of the caravan. Frenchy had spotted three horses hobbled on the far side of the small clearing and the fringed buckskin on the back of a man packing wood to the secluded campsite.

"Well, what have we here? Looks like somebody is preparing a meal for company."

Without hesitation, Frenchy ordered his followers to position themselves for his planned arrival as unexpected and unwanted guests of the camp. Motioning the directions, he ordered his men, "Horse Catcher and Walks, you two drop back and down the tree covered slope, then around the right side thru that brush covered draw. We'll give you time to make it behind that camp, then we'll come in thru the clearing. You'll know when to strike, but don't hit too quick." With a nod of understanding, the two dropped from their horses and quietly disappeared.

Turning to the Gros Ventre he said, "Yellow Cloud, you wait here with that one pack horse we have left and don't come up till we holler fer ya."

Looking at the rest of the pack, he said, "Check your pistols and get ready." Then looking at Rosencrantz, "Uh, maybe you better stay here with Cloud, you ain't movin' too fast."

"That suits me just fine. I wouldn't want to hinder you none," replied the fat man with a grin that acknowledged his cowardly character.

"All right, you two follow me. Try to look friendly and harmless. Remember, we're just lookin' for our friends."

With a kick of his heels to the side of his gray, Frenchy led the predators forward. As they approached the camp, they hailed the strangers, "Hallooo the camp. Can we come in?"

A raspy voice called back, "Keep yore hands clear of any weapons and step down off them horses. Then you can come in, if yore peaceable. We'll kill ya, if ya ain't."

"Whoa, now. We're friendly and harmless. Just passin' thru and thot we might share a little coffee and vittles. We got some fresh meat, but we're all outta coffee beans," said Frenchy with a wide smile masking his intentions. The three men had stepped down, but kept their weapons within reach, an action that was not missed by the camp dwellers.

As the group approached the newly started fire, Frenchy noted the heavy packs, pelt bundles, and ample supplies of their hosts. A second man, also in fringed buckskins, stepped from behind a dead snag of a tree with his rifle held on the trespassers. Without speaking and with a simple nod of his balding head, the trapper approached the fire ring. Most of the men stepped a little cautiously and gathered around the fire to take seats on rocks and a stump, while Hawg dragged the hind quarter of the mule deer left from the previous nights feast, from the back of Frenchy's horse. With the visitors now separated from their weapons, the trappers relaxed a bit, and began a conversation with their visitors. As the bearded and bulk of a mountain man opened his mouth to speak, the whisper of arrows was followed by the solid thunk as both arrows sunk deep into the torsos of the two friendly trappers who wouldn't live long enough to regret their hospitality. As the second of the two men tried to cry out, he discharged his rifle into the ground and grunted as he fell face down in the dirt. The first man had seated himself on a log and had bent to grab another log to feed the fire, twisted and fell with his back in the flames.

"Pull him outta there before he starts stinkin'" ordered Frenchy to no one in particular. Hawg jumped to do his bidding and grabbed an ankle of the man and pulled the body into the nearby trees. As he returned, the two Arapaho had already seated themselves by the fire and cut slabs from the venison haunch to ready their meal and without waiting for an invitation, Hawg followed suit. The kid was disappointed he didn't get to be a part of the killing, so he stepped to the edge of the clearing and firing his pistol in the air, he hollered for the two stragglers to join them.

As the pack took possession of the camp, they unloaded the packs and gear, dropping all to add to the piles of plunder. Frenchy ordered the kid to take the horses to the clearing, hobble them, and return with some firewood as the others prepared their bedrolls. Almon and Yellow Cloud had joined the circle and prepared their meal as well. With a look of revulsion, Almon struggled to drag the body of the smaller trapper from the only remaining area for his bedroll. Not wanting to make his bed on the blood stained dirt patch, he began kicking dirt and dust on the gory evidence of the killing. A chorus of complaint arose from the group and Frenchy yelled, "Hey, careful there fat boy, you're kicking up too much dust."

"Yeah, yeah, what do you care. It's just somebody's blood. Somebody that don't mean nothin' to nobody anymore," complained Rosencrantz.

"What got into you? When did you hatch a conscience? You might not have killed that one, but you're no better than the rest of us, so quit preachin' at us, or you might just join those two," ordered Frenchy.

Knowing he had stepped a little too far into the area of stupid stunts, Almon bit his lower lip to keep himself from answering Frenchy and probably getting himself killed. He knew life held little value for the little Frenchman, and his Napoleonic attitude could easily give rise to his dangerous retribution. Rosencrantz knew Frenchy better than most, as he had been ordered to accompany him on this slave catching, reward seeking, bloody trip through the wilderness. Almon had been employed by Frenchy's brother-in-law, Isaiah Wilmington, one of the first plantation owners and slave holders in the Kentucky area. When Ezekiel the slave had escaped, Wilmington blamed Ezekiel for the uprising of the slaves in the area that mimicked the slave revolts in the Carolinas at the time. Although Ezekiel didn't take any slaves with him, many followed him in the escape. Because of his loss, Wilmington put his brother-in-law, Lucuque DuBois, on the track with promises of bounties and rewards for each slave returned or killed. Rosencrantz was ordered to accompany him because Wilmington experience with Frenchy had taught him his brother-in-law was totally dishonest and untrustworthy. Rosencrantz' assignment was to verify every action that demanded payment.

Frenchy's physical limitations fueled his attitude of hatred and evil. With one leg slightly deformed and shorter, he compensated with built-up soles on his boots of three inches of laminated wood. This helped him walk with less of a limp, and added to his arsenal of weapons that were put to use in his outbursts of anger. It was that anger that bred caution in the mind of Rosencrantz and limited his response to quiet affirmations to Frenchy's orders.

The Indians always rose before the dawn and this morning found the two Arapaho gathering the horses to the campsite and Yellow Cloud stoking the fire in anticipation of a morning meal. The movement brought the lazy crew of white men to wakefulness as each stirred from their blankets. None of the pack was in any hurry to get on the trail and each one lazily attended to their assigned camp chores.

While the others slept, Yellow Cloud had slipped from the camp and traveled the back trail by moonlight to check for any pursuit. Now, as Frenchy returned to the fire, Yellow Cloud gave his report. "We are followed."

"Are you sure?" responded Frenchy, realizing his statement was an insult to the Gros Ventre. Yellow Cloud just looked at him without response.

"How many, and how far back are they?" asked Frenchy.

"I only saw three horses. They are less than one day behind, still high up on the trail."

"Are you sure they're after us? Not just some other trappers or such like?" as he looked askance to the Indian.

Cloud simply looked at him, slowly nodding his head in affirmation. No other emotion or response was required. The stoic Indian now left the problem with this little man that led the group. Frenchy stood, looked at Cloud, then to the men, and walked to the opening of the clearing, looking to their back trail as if he could see the pursuers. Reaching at his feet, he retrieved a twig of almost 2 feet in length and as he began to pace the distance between the sentinel pines at the clearing entrance, he repeatedly slapped his leg to further kindle his anger and frustration.

"We ain't gonna run from no two or three Indians on some stupid revenge hunt. We will take care of them right here," he declared, with the seeds of another plan for ambush and blood began to grow in his twisted mind.

To Keep a Promise

Chapter Nine: Blood

WHAT STARTED THE ARGUMENT was unknown and unimportant but the level of the ruckus now rose to an excited pitch that the verbal battle echoed off the wall of tall pines. The clamor was loud enough to alarm the camp dwellers causing each to react. Jeremiah's bare muscled arm stretched from his buffalo robe blanket to snatch at his rifle while Waters sat up with sleep-laden eyes searching for the source of disturbance. Shield's response was the quickest and deadliest as he grabbed his brass and steel headed tomahawk and with one easy throw to the mark sunk the wide blade deep into the log by the fire. The two chattering chipmunks disappeared with one diving into his hole in the log and the other scrambling around the base of the nearby tree.

The still glowing coals of the night fire were just enough to illuminate the now whiskered face of Jeremiah and revealed a surprised and slightly angered grump that exclaimed, "Whooaa, Shield, remind me not to wake you up too early!"

Shield's response was no more than a mocking grunt as he rolled over and back under his blankets. With a muffled command he asked, "Why don't you stoke up the fire and get some bacon goin' so we'll have a reason to face the cold morning?"

"What! You don't want to argue with me like your new found friends did? I know they scared you wide awake!"

"Will you two brave warriors quit acting like those chipmunks and get my meal going?" interjected Waters, as she giggled at the two still tangled in their blankets.

It was good to start the day with the easy banter of trusted friends for each knew the coming days would provide little opportunity to enjoy this well-tested friendship. Jeremiah kicked aside his buffalo robe and stood to his feet surveying the supply packs and finding the parfleche with the needed provisions, stooped to start the newly assigned task. Reaching first for the blue enamel coffee pot, then the bag of coffee beans, he strolled to the nearby stream for water. Returning to find the others rolling bedrolls and arranging packs and gear, Jeremiah set the pot on the large stone near the fire. Placing a small handful of the coffee beans on the stone and using the butt end of his knife handle, he crushed the beans, scooped the coffee to his palm and dropped it into the coffee pot. Waters joined him with the small frying pan and several freshly cut strips of salt pork and placed the pan with the pork on the space between two stones at the edge of the fire. She reached back to the packs, retrieved three pieces of fry-bread to warm with the salt-pork.

With the gray light of early morning slowly making it way up the Eastern sky, the darkness started its retreat. The caravan of young warriors began their descent of the lower timber covered trail of the Northeast side of Two Bears Pass. With brief glimpses of the horizon to their right, the orange and red colors were soon displaced with the full brightness of morning. The trail had become wider, the timber more sparse, and the slope of the mountainside considerably less. Waters called to Shield, now in the lead, "Brother, wait a bit," then moved her sorrel beside his paint gelding. "We need some meat and I want to see what that small meadow might be hiding," as she motioned with a nod of her head towards the left of the trail.

"You take my mare and I'll meet you at the bottom."

Shield turned to look at Jeremiah as if to ask his opinion. White Wolf just shrugged his shoulders and yielded to Shield. As Shield looked at his sister, he could not find a reason to disagree and with a simple nod, took the lead rope of her mare. Waters dropped to the side of the trail and bent her bow to stretch the bowstring to ready herself for the hunt. Without another look she slipped into the shadows of the cluster of spruce trees. Shield and Jeremiah prompted their horses to continue with a simple leg squeeze to the horses ribs as the riders settled into the saddle packs for the comfortable ride to the bottom of the pass trail.

It took but a few strides before Waters melted into the woods, her buckskin attire and dark skin and hair were perfect camouflage for the fall colors of the forest. With the stealth of a predator she glided noiselessly through the pines, the windfall logs, and the contrasting quakies. Following a faint game path that paralleled the trail traveled by Shield and White Wolf, Waters had traversed the down sloping trail about a quarter of a mile when she was startled by a large bull elk busting out of the brush. With his antlers laid back on his broad mud colored back, his reddish brown chest parted the oak brush as Waters brought up her bow. Taking a spread legged stance she drew the flint bladed arrow to its full length, sighted along the shaft and prepared to loose the messenger of death. *"Wait, what startled him? He's too far away from the trail for Shield to have spooked him. What, or who was it?"* Releasing the draw, she relaxed her stance to again stand in the shadows of the nearby copse. The look on the face of the elk, whites of his eyes showing, mouth open and drawing wind, tongue lolling out with slobbers flying revealed fear had caused his flight. Slowly letting out her captured breath, Waters turned her head to the darker timber, looking for the cause of the Bull Elk's alarm. *"I would rather let that one live another day, than to*

71

miss a bigger challenge, like another grizzly or the renegades in ambush," she thought.

Now her stalk of a hunt became the stealth of the hunted. Not knowing what to expect but preparing for anything that had reason to hide in the dark shadows, she stepped lightly down the game trail. Never turning a stone, breaking a twig, or crushing a leaf, the maiden warrior blended with the colors and sounds of the woods. From first the tall pine, to the fallen log, to the thicket of brush, her shadow moved without disturbing the stillness of eons. Knowing she had to move quickly because of the winding trail of the packhorses and warriors and wanting to stay any impending danger, she was momentarily careless. The lichen covered piece of shale that she thought would bear her weight betrayed her and sent her sprawling in the trail. The fall alerted the waiting renegade Arapaho Horse Catcher, who had hidden behind the trunk of the large dark green and brown fir with overhanging branches that perfectly concealed him from the trail. The fallen girl was behind him and to his right, causing him to have to spin farther, plant his feet and draw his bow and feathered shaft. Because she was on his off side, the momentary delay enabled her to roll behind the nearby buckbrush. As she drew herself to her knees, one swift motion brought up her bow, arrow, and she drew to its full length. With instinct rather than sight, she let the arrow fly. Passing in the air, Horse Catcher's arrow sought its mark as Waters' shaft whispered it message of doom.

Horse Catcher choked on his cry of death as the arrow entered the base of his throat and passed the full length of the shaft through his neck. The arrow stopping as the feathers hindered the piercing, the renegade appeared to have a necklace of feathers for his last journey. With little sound, his knees buckled and he dropped to the ground. Unable to see any other attackers, Waters lifted her voice in a warning cry, "Aaaiiiiieeeeeeeee" knowing her brother would hear the cry and the echo as the warning traveled unhindered down the wooded hillside. Hearing the cry, both Shield and Wolf

72

dropped to the neck of their mounts, then rolled to the ground in one fluid motion. As Shield rolled to the side of his pinto he felt a tug on his buckskin tunic. When he hit the ground, he knew an arrow unsuccessfully sought to draw blood from his side. Shield quietly motioned to Wolf the direction of the attacker or attackers but Wolf had already spotted the movement and was bringing his rifle to his shoulder. To attract the attention of the attacker, Shield made a short cry and kicked the bush behind him. The slight move made by Yellow Cloud to adjust his aim brought the attacker into the view of Wolf just long enough for him to squeeze the front thin trigger sending the lead ball in a cloud of white smoke to tell the renegade of his mistake.

Waters ran to the trail to the aid of her warrior brothers and was quickly at their side.

"Are there any others?" Shield inquired of his sister.

"I killed one but I see no more," she replied. Then after a short pause, she said, "Brother, he was of the People." The Arapaho, like most Indians, referred to themselves as *The People.* Shield was surprised at this revelation. As his brow wrinkled and his eyebrows dropped low over his eyes, he said, "Did you know him?"

"No, he wasn't from our village. I have not seen him before," she responded.

"I believe the one over there was a Gros Ventre. I don't understand why they were together and also with the white men. Maybe they both were exiles." When a member of the village of any tribe refused to abide by the tribal laws and would not make right as required of any wrongdoing, the offender would often be exiled from the village and even the tribe. Often these exiles banded together to form a new village or even a new tribe. The Gros Ventre were thought to have become a tribe under just such circumstances. However, for those of different tribes to be allied together with renegade whites, was not a common or accepted thing.

Jeremiah stepped to their side and said, "Well, whatever they were, they ain't no more. But what we got to be concerned about, is are there any more?"

"We are almost to the clearing below, let us go nearer and see what or who is there," counseled Shield. Without further discussion, the trio led the horses to the edge of the trees and tethered them out of sight. Staying in the shadows and behind the larger trees, Shield and his two companions surveyed the clearing. Immediately spotting the three horses tethered to the far edge, it was evident that a campsite was just inside the cover of the pines. Unable to see any activity or other sign of anyone inhabiting the camp, the three drew back into the shadows to formulate their plan.

"Well, we know there were at least three, because of the horses. But, we're not sure if the two we did in are part of the three. Also, we don't know for sure these are the ones we're after," stated Jeremiah.

"There were few tracks at other sites to be certain of these two. We should expect there are more," mused Shield.

"But what should we do? We can't just wait here," said Waters.

"Well, here's what I'm thinkin,' how 'bout we do this. Shield, you and Waters work your way around the downstream side of this clearing. Waters, you find a good spot to the downhill side of the camp and wait. Shield, you continue to make your way around the uphill side and come at the camp from those quakies over there," said Jeremiah as he motioned with his arm.

"I'll give you all time to get where you're goin' and then I'll just ride in from here and hello the camp, like I was just lookin' for coffee or sumpin. Then the two of you come a little closer and be ready for me to open the dance."

Shield considered the plan of White Wolf as he lowered his eyes to the ground. Then turning to Waters with his eyebrows raised to solicit her thoughts, he motioned to her with an open palm. Without any comment, she stepped out to begin

74

her trek to her position. Shield turned to Wolf, shrugged his shoulders, and followed his sister.

While Jeremiah bided his time, he re-loaded his rifle and carefully ensured his flint was solid and sound, the frizzen moved smoothly and his wiping stick secure. He also filled the frizzen with flash powder and made ready to leave. Before mounting, he looked to the hillside across the meadow and its slight cover of fir and aspen. With a careful scan, he sought any movement or any sign that would give away his fellow conspirators. Reassured, he made firm the tethers of Shield's and Waters horses, mounted his appaloosa and started for the clearing. Approaching the hobbled horses of the renegades, they lifted their heads and whinnied a greeting to his stud. Jeremiah moved to the uphill side of the grassy plot where the horses grazed and keeping his eyes on the campsite, he searched for some sign of any occupants. He hollered the greeting, "Helloo the camp. I'm comin' in." There was no response, no movement to be seen. As he stepped down from his mount, he called out again, "Hello, anyone around?" Again, no response.

The crack of the pistol barely preceded the whistle of the .50 caliber ball by Jeremiah's left ear. Although he dismounted with his rifle in hand, it was still in the leather sheath. The pistol shot had spooked his horse that now pulled at the reins gripped in Jeremiah's hand. Spinning on the ball of his right foot, he pushed away from his struggling horse, leveling the rifle at the mountain of a man exploding from the shadows and charging directly at him. With the bellow of a raging bull on the prod, waving an axe in his right hand above his head, the smoking pistol in his uplifted left hand and his boots stomping dust clouds around his legs, Hawg's face was covered with the blue of the veins bent on exploding as he charged to murder this man before him. Jeremiah pulled the trigger on the sheathed flintlock that exploded in a cloud of thunder and smoke through the hole in the end of the sheath made by the spiraling .54 slug. The smoke belched backwards around

White Wolf's hand as his eyes were filled with nothing but the bushy bearded monster bearing down on him. Jeremiah saw the red blossom dead center of Hawg's chest and thought, "He's dead and he's still comin.'"

Two arrows buried themselves in the sides of the charging behemoth without effect. Before he took two more steps, a third arrow found its mark in his neck, but the maniacal beast did not stammer in his step. As he reached Jeremiah, the monster brought his axe down with the strength of a man that did not know he was dying but sought to bring death to another. The blow glanced off the side of Jeremiah's head, tearing a piece of scalp with it, then continued to the shoulder of the terrified victim. The head of the axe buried itself deep in the fleshly muscle of his left arm and shoulder but with such a force, both slayer and victim tumbled to the dirt. The weight of Hawg pinned Jeremiah to the ground and robbed him of the strength even to draw breath. Shield and Waters pushed and pulled the pile of dead meat from their fellow warrior and sought to ensure that Jeremiah still lived. Wolf lay still, not breathing, eyes staring without seeing.

"Wolf, don't you die on me! I won't let you!" screamed Waters to the prostrate form of her secret love. With a deep sucking draw of air that filled his empty lungs, Jeremiah's eyes widened and he turned a smile to Waters.

"You won't let me? Well, that's good, cuz I ain't got no plans of dyin' just yet."

The blood was now flowing from his wound and around the still buried blade of the axe. The blade was held fast by the broken collar bone and the muscle in the shoulder. As Waters carefully examined the wound and applied pressure with a piece of linen grabbed from Wolf's possibles bag, without even asking Wolf, she grabbed the handle of the axe and swiftly pulled it upward to remove it from the wound and bone. The sudden action, pain, and blood loss caused Jeremiah to drop into unconsciousness.

Chapter Ten: Healing

AS THE SETTING SUN painted the backside of the Abasaroka mountain range, the darkness began to drop across the meadow and surrounding trees that sheltered their campsite. The body of the huge renegade now lay in a shallow grave away from the camp and was covered with some rocks and branches in an attempt to prevent any scavengers from coming around uninvited. Shield had fashioned the dome shaped hut by bending over several aspen saplings, securing them together and weaving many pine boughs through the lattice work walls and roof. Waters made Jeremiah as comfortable as possible, then rummaged through his medicine pack and hers as well, searching for whatever could be used to minister to the wounded warrior that lay at her feet. Not finding what she needed, she made a quick foraging journey to the nearby stream and surrounding area to gain what she deemed necessary. Without any additional delay, she began her treatment.

Shield laid aside the blanket covering the opening to the hut and bent to look inside. The small fire near the entrance, illumined the interior. "How is he?" inquired Shield.

"He's still bleeding too much. I thought that compress would stop it, but now I'm going to have to sew his wound together."

"What do you need me to do?"

"After I get it cleaned more, you will need to hold him down."

Before she renewed the cleaning of the gash from the axe, she prepared a poultice to cover the wound. Shield watched as Waters worked to blend the age old remedy. Small willow twigs were laid side by side on the stone then pounded into a stringy pad. Moving that aside, she took a small handful of Yarrow stems and a small piece of root and a few blossoms, then rolling these under the smaller stone to crush them to a pulp, she then pushed that to the side with the willow. Next, she picked up a handful of dried and hardened chunks of Douglas Fir sap, then ground them to a powder. Putting the Yarrow pulp on top of the willow pad, then sprinkling the powdered sap on top of that, she set it aside to apply later.

"You remind me of our father, Black Kettle. You have always shared his Healer's touch," mused Shield. "Maybe you should become a recognized healer, our village will always need a healer."

"I once thought White Wolf would follow our Father, but when the council wouldn't allow it, I lost interest in doing that work as well," replied Waters.

She turned her attention to her patient, removing his bandage. The wound was deep and jagged and still bled. She felt the underlying collar bone, and commented, "Pulling out that axe also pulled the bone back in place. I think it will heal well." She began cleaning the wound by dipping a rag in the basin of water, wrung it out and washed the deep bleeding gash. Jeremiah stirred but didn't regain consciousness.

"I'm going to do this quickly, so come in and hold him down," she ordered. Then reaching for needle and thread she had taken from Jeremiah's pack, she began. With deft fingers, she pulled the wound together with eight loops of the heavy thread, pulled it tight and tied it off. The bleeding had stanched, but was not completely stopped. The attending healer picked up the prepared pad of willow and yarrow and fir sap, placed it with the sap side against the wound then pressed it down firmly. She covered it with a leather patch, pulled a leather strap under his shoulder and back to make the bandage secure. During the entire process, Jeremiah only stirred slightly and emitted a low moan, then returned to his unconscious state.

"He's going to need rest and nourishment. Tomorrow, you'll need to get us some fresh meat. Wolf will need that to regain his strength and to make his blood strong again," said Waters.

"I will rise early and maybe get something coming down for a morning drink at the stream. There are plenty of deer in the area, a few elk also," replied Shield.

The shelter was of ample size for the two to spread their sleeping blankets to either side of Jeremiah. Shield placed his nearest the opening and opposite the small fire then readily wrapped himself in the warmth and faced the opening. Waters laid her blankets beside Jeremiah and lay next to her patient. The trials and stress of the day soon overtook the trio and the sounds of sleep filled the hut.

The low growl swelled in volume to a sudden yip and snapping of jaws that rolled Shield from his blankets. Grabbing his nearby bow, he used his foot and left arm to bend the red willow to enable him to attach the bowstring and make his bow ready. Snatching three arrows on his way out of the hut opening, he then searched the moonlit camp and nearby trees for the source of the sound that disturbed his slumber. A short distance into the trees, where Shield had disposed of the body of the renegade, the growling and yipping continued. Bending to his attack stance, Shield notched an arrow to his bowstring and stealthily neared the conflict.

Two large wolves, the smaller silver and black wolf faced toward Shield but held its eyes on the larger solid black wolf that faced its smaller opponent. Sensing something behind him, the black whirled with his head dropped low, teeth bared, slobbers stringing from its lolling tongue, and the moon mirrored in its eyes. If ever evil had a face, this was it. The stare momentarily petrified Shield as he admired the raw beauty of the larger than normal grave robber. Putting aside their argument, the silver wolf slowly stepped to the side of the black growling beast. Now the pair fastened their malevolent stare on this intruder and with rumbling growls from deep in their chests, the two began a slow stalk of the man. Almost in unison, each paw lifted, moved forward and silently found its place. Then the next pace brought them closer and closer, with their teeth bared and drool spilling from their jowls and their eyes never losing focus on their intended prey.

A shout of "Shoot!" from his side broke the trance that held Shield and with a full draw of his bow, he let fly the arrow toward its mark. Waters also sent an arrow to the pair but both shafts embedded themselves in the chest of the black dropping him as he exhaled his life with a short whimper. The untouched silver denizen of the night turned and disappeared in the darkness.

The next morning, Shield was successful with his morning hunt and soon returned to the campsite to find Jeremiah struggling to sit up in his tangle of blankets and a complaining Waters.

Trying to push her patient down, she said, "You have to rest. Don't move around like that. You will start bleeding again." Scowling at Jeremiah, Waters tried to pen him down with her stare.

"Uh, no, there are some things you can't help me with. Now help me up, so I can go to the trees to take care of business," he said with a mischievous grin spreading across his face.

He was a little unsteady as he made his way to the opening, then stooping to exit, he reached back in to Waters and sought her steadying arm for his first uncertain steps. When it was apparent that Jeremiah could make his own way and didn't really want her help, Waters turned to join Shield and help with the preparation of his morning kill. The deer hung from the overarching large branch of the ponderosa and Shield was pulling the hide down the inverted carcass. The two worked quickly together cutting the back strap, the shoulders and the hind quarters into strips for smoking. Cutting enough of the loin for their noon meal, Waters laid the cut steaks aside and prepared to smoke the other cuts.

With oft-practiced moves, Waters assembled a smoke rack of green willow shafts and rawhide strips. The rack, holding the strips of meat, would overhang the fire of coals, and be mostly covered to contain the smoke and preserve the meat. Usually the covering would be a heavy blanket or other robe type covering, but Waters was using the fresh pelt from the slain black wolf. She had already scraped it clean of flesh and rubbed the brain matter into the under side of the hide and now the smoke would further the tanning process to make a soft pelt for the winter. This preparation process usually took several days, but Waters knew time was in short supply and she was determined not to lose out on another pelt. Leaving the big fur of the Grizzly was enough of a loss and she wouldn't leave another behind.

Jeremiah had returned and was now reclined against a log near the fire and was eagerly devouring some jerky and left over pan bread. The pallor of his face told the story of his loss of blood and his scarcity of movement emphasized his weakness. Shield had joined him by the fire and sat on the larger of the two stones nearby. "My brother's face looks like the pelt of a mountain goat but your whiskers make you look like the bear. I've never seen both at the same time," observed Shield. "I think you need some of Water's pemmican stew to bring back the brother I know."

"Well, why don't you just go and get me some of the berries I need to make it then. If I know you, you won't be too shy about eating that stew yourself," directed Laughing

Waters. Pulling himself erect, Shield stooped to pick up an empty parfleche and left, dragging his feet and muttering something about woman's work. Waters was anxious to get started with the task of replenishing their food supplies for the remainder of the quest, but knew the immediate need was to do everything she could to hasten the healing of Jeremiah. Using the larger pot that had been part of the left-behind packs of the renegades, she cut up some of the fresh venison and placed the pieces, fat side down, into the pot to start the nourishing stew. With the pot resting over the space between two stones, the flames licked the bottom with the fat-melting heat. It wasn't long before the return of Shield brought the needed ingredients to complete the stew. Waters was pleased as she rummaged through the parfleche, picking first some cranberries, then rose hips and a few huckleberries, a handful of chokecherries and then some onions to complete the stew makings. Washing off the selected additions, she dropped them into the pot with some fresh spring water and let the stew begin its work.

She was thankful for the harvest of berries at the hand of Shield. The remainder of his gleanings would be used to make the pemmican. Waters would use some of the smoked meat and pounding it together with the berries, her stone worktable would yield a nourishing and long lasting sustenance for the journey. The days of rest and recuperation for Jeremiah would be days well spent by Waters preparing the meats and other foodstuffs that would make their travel more sustainable.

Chapter Eleven: Yellowstone

BREAKING CAMP after three days of recovery for Jeremiah, was a welcomed activity for all. The lack of travel of the previous days gave time to restore the provisions of smoked meat, jerky, and pemmican. With the additional packs and horses from the slain renegades, the packing of the extra supplies was made easier. The trio had doubled up the packs on their own horses after losing the one pack animal to the grizzly attack, and the additions to their caravan gave considerable relief to the task.

During the layover, Shield had scouted the tracks and trail of the renegades and he now led the way on the descending trail. The tall pines and aspen gave way to scattered juniper and twisted pinion as the trail dropped into the rolling plains East of the mountains. The travel was easier and they covered more miles than previous days. Caution was still necessary due to the rolling hills and draws of the area. It was easy to look to the horizon and think the plain was flat and devoid of cover, but the rolling hills easily hid the many draws and gullies that harbored small spring fed streams, or storm washed and adobe mud covered shallows. These depressions would easily hide game animals and hunting parties of the Crow

83

nation. The Arapaho and Crow nations were not blood enemies, but the occasional raid to the others camp for horses and honor was not an unusual event. With this always in mind, Shield usually chose the trail that led through the bottom of these draws and canyons. It was easy to follow the trail of the renegades without having to travel in the same path. To outline oneself on the horizon was to ask for an attack. An occasional scout about the area would reaffirm the trail they followed was the same.

As the three hunters-of-men approached a small clearing surrounded by tall cottonwoods, it was decided to make a meal stop and give the horses a bit of graze and rest. The grass spread from the small spring-fed pool that was sufficient for water for the animals and to refill their water bags. Shield gathered an armload of dry firewood and started a small fire while Jeremiah let himself down on a blanket spread on a corner of the grass patch. He was annoyed that the shoulder wound wasn't healing faster, but Waters applications of poultices and bandages were doing their work. The soreness seemed to be a little less, but the collar bone restricted his movement as well as sending a stabbing pain when he tried to do too much.

"Those we seek are following this river that flows from the yellow stone. This is new country for me and I do not know where they go," stated Shield speaking to Jeremiah. "I have not seen it, but I am told this river joins another larger one many days to the NorthEast."

"When Ezekiel and I went to the Rendezvous I remember some of the men talking about a new trading post the American Fur company was puttin' up where those two rivers meet. I think they called it Fort Union, but I'm not real sure about that," replied Jeremiah.

"They have stayed on the North side of the river and do not hurry. We should be near them in three or four days, maybe longer. I have not crossed any sign of others, but we must be watchful for the Crow and soon the Blackfeet," cautioned Shield.

"Well, we've made purty good time so far, and if the weather don't do us in, we should make even better time in the next few days. Us bein' able to switch horses ever now and then helps that a bunch," mused White Wolf.

"Yes, but more horses leave more sign. And more horses are tempting to hunting parties," added Shield, again sounding the warning for caution. Shield was one that carefully planned, cautiously proceeded, and as a result he was always successful at whatever he undertook. Jeremiah had always appreciated Shield and his concern, but because Jeremiah's way was to charge ahead and let the details sort themselves out, the two friends often locked horns.

As the two men, typical of most groups of men, discussed the problems and needs of the day, Waters had finished cooking the noon meal. She had prepared a sort of hash with smoked venison, wild onions, and breadroot or prairie turnip and summoned the men to partake. Quickly prepared, quickly consumed, and quickly forgotten without a word of gratitude given, and Waters carefully pondered her response and the timing of the soon-to-be learned lesson for the two warriors.

Shield again led the way of the caravan of six horses, the three mounts with Shield, Jeremiah and Waters, and the three that doubled as pack horses and relief mounts. Jeremiah twisted around in his saddle to observe their back-trail and the sign they were leaving. With his weight in the left stirrup and his right leg crooked across the seat, he held the saddle horn with his left hand, cradled his rifle in the crook of his right arm, and surveyed the receding foothills and plains. Letting his gaze fall to Waters, his eyes and his thoughts lingered. This woman, who just days ago was a girl that he chased through the woods, was now a beautiful vision in the simple attire of beaded buckskins and with straight black hair trailing in the slight breeze. With his mind distracted, Jeremiah turned back to again watch the trail between the ears of his mount, but the image of Waters obscured his vision and his thoughts. With the easy walking gait of the horses, it was common to mentally drift to other times and places. These quiet times allowed Jeremiah to contemplate the quest they were on and more, especially the future and Waters and what would happen after the completion of this journey. Was there a future for the two of them? Would she consider him as a possible life-long mate? Is that what he wanted?

Fortunately for Jeremiah, on the trail most horses have more sense than their riders, and when Shield stopped his mount and pack-horse, Jeremiah's stopped of its own accord. The ceasing of the rocking motion brought Jeremiah back to awareness. He immediately lifted his eyes to Shield to see what prompted the stop, then seeing him eyeing the distant rolling hills to the North, Jeremiah turned and sought the source of Shield's caution. Seeing nothing, he turned to Shield and with a motion of his hand, indicated his question. Shield responded with signs indicating a party of six warriors, probably Crow, approaching their general direction. Dropping to his horse's neck and with a leg squeeze, Shield moved to a small depression between the river and the trail. Jeremiah and Waters quickly followed in the same manner.

Shield stepped from his mount, handed the lead ropes to Jeremiah and made his way to the crest of the small rise that shielded them from the Crow party. As he neared the crest, he dropped to his hands and knees and crawled the rest of the way to view the progress of the hunting party. Dropping to his belly, he continued to watch the party of braves for any sign that they had seen Shield and his companions. Without changing direction, the trail the Crow were following would take them nearer the river and the trail at a point near where the trio had traveled before their nooning. Shield returned to his fellow warriors.

"They did not see us, but they will cross our trail before long. We must put as much distance between us as we can and find a place better suited for a fight," stated Shield, then

86

continued. "We will follow this low ground as far as we can, but we will travel fast. Check the packs before we leave."

With everything tightened up and secured, the trio kicked off in a lope with each rider straining at the lead rope of the pack horses. One hand on the reins, one on the lead rope, and legs gripping tightly, the riders followed single file at the ground-eating pace set by Shield. Alternating between a lope and a walk, the miles melted away under the hooves of the tiring horses. Because the packhorses were well loaded, at this pace it would be fruitless to change horses for increased stamina. When the group again slowed to a walk, Shield indicated with his raised hand they were nearing a possible camp site.

The rolling terrain had increased on the uphill side with hills that dropped off with staggered sandstone shelves forming a cliff-like precipice that made possible shelter. Shield led them beside one uprising cliff that bent around the shoulder of the hill and back into a secluded draw. The overhanging stones would provide shelter from anything above them, and the mouth of the draw was small enough to be easily protected. Riding into the opening, they observed the combination of twisted juniper and sage-brush that littered the floor of the small canyon, occasional patches of yucca tried in vain to climb the sandstone walls. Shield indicated the larger overhang for the use of their camp, then dropping from his mount, he led the horses to an area behind the juniper that had a bit of wheat grass and a little gramma grass for the horses. Waters saw her opportunity and walking to the overhang, she sat down on a large stone in the quickly darkening shade and waited for the men.

Jeremiah and Shield tethered the horses with enough lead rope to allow them to graze, removed the packs and gear, and brought the necessary accouterments to the campsite. Seeing Waters sitting idly on the stone, the men looked at her, at each other, and with quizzical looks, open arms and upturned hands, asked "What?" Normally, Waters would have gathered firewood and started the fire for the last meal of the day, but nothing was done. She leaned back with her hands clasped in front of one knee and the other leg stretching to the ground, she said, "Yeah, I'm hungry too." It took a little while, but the men finally understood. Without a word, Jeremiah went in search of firewood and Shield began to rummage through the packs to find something to prepare for the meal.

After struggling to down a meal of a few pieces of fried salt-pork, left-over pan bread dipped in the grease and some strips of smoked venison warmed over the open fire, all of which were better before the would-be cooks did their part, the travelers prepared to turn in for the night. Jeremiah and Shield agreed to split the night on watch and Jeremiah took his place for the first shift. Shield and Waters rolled in their blankets by the dwindling light of the fire. Although she tried to stifle it, Shield heard the snicker emanating from the blankets of Waters. With a grunt, Shield rolled over turning his back to his roguish sister and sought the escape of sleep before his watch for the night.

Chapter Twelve: Ambush

AFTER THE SNOW in the mountains and the frost in the lowlands, the travelers were enjoying Indian Summer. It was a time of warm days and cool nights that sometimes happens in the late fall or early winter months following the first cold snap. It was unusual for this weather phenomenon to occur this late in the year, and it was welcomed by everyone but the early winter hibernating animals.

Jeremiah and company were on the trail early and enjoyed the sunrise over the far distant hills. The red colors of the cloud covered sky warned of a possible weather change, but the travelers were subject to both the terrain and the temperature and would not allow their thoughts to linger on that which they could not change. Jeremiah led out on the path while Shield brought up the rear. Shield wanted to be in position to check on any followers as he was not certain that the previously spotted Crow hunting party didn't pick up their trail. While Waters held the rocking chair position in the middle of the caravan, each one of the travelers trailed a pack horse and the six horses left easy-to-follow tracks.

The horses quickly settled into their steady rocking gait and the hip-rolling, leather creaking, dust-stirring movement lulled Jeremiah into a melancholy state of introspection. *How quickly things change in this life. Just a couple of weeks ago I didn't have a care in the world and spent my days enjoying our work and spending time with my friends. Now I'm on a vengeance quest, something I had never even thought of before. But is it the right thing? What would Ezekiel think of this, would he think vengeance is the thing to do? He always said to do the right thing and treat others with respect and all, but this bunch murdered him! Justice has to be done; I can't just let them get away with it. And what about the gold we had worked so hard for, the gold he was going to use to free his family? I promised I would help him free them, and this is the only way I know to get that done. Nothing is more important than keeping your promises, Mom used to always say that was the measure of man.*

Although his thoughts were scampering about, Jeremiah was still watchful on the trail. As he looked to the horizon he took in the gently rolling plains and the light brown uninterrupted color that held few shadows and no variation. He noticed the cholla cactus that grew in abundance and always seemed to be in groupings. The dead cholla had a look of braided wood in a lattice work pattern with diamond shaped holes in the hollow branches. A few of the living plants clung selfishly to a rare pink or yellow late blossom. Next to the trail were patches of the prickly pear cactus with its many sharp needles catching an occasional small tumbleweed. As other areas in the plains, in the Spring this now monotonous area would be splashed with color from blooming cactus and many other plants like the bright orange Indian paintbrush and the smiling yellow sunflower. But now Jeremiah searched in vain for any color to lift his spirit. He chuckled at the twisting and scampering lizard as it ran from the trail into a nearby sagebrush. Lifting his eyes to the sky and shielding them from the sun, he was unsuccessful in his search for any bird in flight. *Maybe it's too far from the nearest tree for a nest. Those cottonwoods down by the river are probably well over a mile from here. You'd think that an Osprey or a hawk would be hunting this area for rabbits or field mice.*

The chuckle of a sage grouse came from behind him, but Jeremiah knew the call was mimicked by Shield. Turning to respond, he saw Shield making signs of immediate danger. Reining his horse back to await Shield, Jeremiah scanned the back trail but saw nothing. In a whisper, Jeremiah said, "Shield, what's the matter?" As Shield sided Jeremiah, he said, "I think it's the Crow, they are following, but I do not think they have seen us. We should find a place to fight, the best would be near the river." He dug his heels in the ribs of his mount to move towards the river, hopeful of finding a place of defense. Being careful not to kick up dust to give away their flight, Jeremiah and Waters closely followed.

Jeremiah watched as Shield and his mount and packhorse disappeared over the bank making an easy-to-follow path for the remainder of the travelers. As they cleared the crest of the bank, Jeremiah could see the wide sandbar with willows against the river bank. He also noted the few cottonwood trees that had yet to reach maturity, but were big enough to provide some cover. The flow of the river was low but rapid as it gurgled on the wide curve away from the sandbar. With a quick glance he noted the distance between the water and the six foot adobe bank was just enough to give protection to the horses. He dropped from his saddle so he and Waters could tether them securely. Grabbing their weapons, the two joined Shield at the riverbank. Jeremiah dropped a knee into the soft soil to gain enough height to look over the crest. Shield said, "We have some time before they get here. We should set an ambush. It is better to attack than wait."

"O.K., what do you have in mind?" responded Jeremiah.

"Well, big brother, you are always good at planning. What do we do?" interjected Waters with an unusual look of concern painted on her face.

After laying out his plan and assigning their positions, Shield stepped out to take his place on the upstream bank.

Jeremiah and Waters looked at each other, shrugged their shoulders and turned to go to their assigned places. Jeremiah turned, "Waters, wait," and stepped to her, putting his arms around her waist and pulling her to his chest. Waters was too surprised to resist as he dropped his head and pressed his lips to hers. As he pulled away, she stood still with a surprised look on her face, and remembered to breathe. Without a word, Jeremiah turned and went to the horses to retrieve his bow and quiver of arrows. Waters put her hand to her lips, watched Jeremiah walk away, then climbed the soft soil of the bank to make her way to her position.

To give the appearance of an established camp, Jeremiah spread some blankets, dropped a couple of packs and saddles, and grabbing some driftwood, started a fire. He made his way through the willows to the base of the cottonwood trees, climbed the cutaway bank for a view of the camp, and prepared his cover. He had a limited view of their back trail and knew he would have to watch the horses for their movement and sounds to betray the presence of intruders. *Well, White Wolf, you've done all you can. Rifle is primed and ready, bow is strung and quiver of arrows handy, two arrows within quick reach. Now, it's just waiting. Shield's plan is a good one; we just need things to go our way.* Another chuckle of a sage grouse gave the warning.

At the top edge of the rolling hump of hill a short distance down the back trail, one Crow warrior bending low to the ground, examined the trail of the three. He turned and motioned to the five others who seemed to rise from the ground below the hill. Too far away to hear, the animated scout made his point regarding the tracks. The warriors approached at a slow walk and spaced themselves out as they neared the riverbank. With four to five bow lengths separating them the warriors fanned out from the leader, a large man with his loose hair fanning back from his face revealing the dark brow and prominent nose arching forward from the deep set eyes that searched the riverbank for any sign of life. None of the party

92

bore war paint, revealing this as a hunting party that thought they stumbled on easy prey with many horses to steal. The rest of the warriors were younger than the leader and the excitement of their coming battle showed on each face as they neared the quarry. At the predetermined sign, they drove their heels in their mounts ribs, screamed their war cry and galloped to the bank and the anticipated battle. Their horses leapt to action and lowered their heads with manes now flying in rippling waves along their necks, muscles corded in strength to send their bodies forward with speed and agility gained from the many buffalo hunts. Guiding their mounts with knee pressure left both hands free for the bow as the chosen weapon of four of the attackers. The leader brandished a massive war club overhead as he anticipated delivering a death blow at the first appearance of his prey.

Jeremiah leaned against the larger of the cottonwoods with his rifle cradled on the webbing between thumb and forefinger and fingers resting against the bark of the tree. As he watched the onslaught of the Crow raiding party, he mentally rechecked his weapon. Hammer cocked, flash pan loaded, frizzen down, triggers set, as he followed the leader with the front brass blade sight aligned with the rear buckhorn sight and both centered on the bead and bone chest plate worn by the man with the fierce countenance. Jeremiah was waiting for his targeted victim to reach the drop off of the riverbank before taking his shot. Only seconds passed and the trail dropped from under the leader's horse, Jeremiah squeezed off his shot. In the brief instant for the hammer to fall, sparks to fly into the flash pan and in turn ignite the powder in the barrel and send the projectile on its way, the second warrior filled the sight picture. Through the white powder cloud, Jeremiah saw the chest of the braided warrior sprout its blossom of red and the startled man tumble backwards off his mount, falling in the path of another warrior and trampled under the feet of his charging horse.

As Shield had instructed, Waters waited until the arched line of warriors neared the riverbank before rising from her position behind the rock outcropping with her bow drawn the full length of the arrow as she sighted on the nearest warrior before letting fly the feathered shaft. Just before releasing, she realized her target was nothing more than a youth, probably twelve winters or less. But he was on a mission of war and death had no age limitation. As she watched the youth grab at the arrow in his side and fall from his pony, Waters had already notched her second arrow and took aim at the next target. Slipping her fingers from the string, she let the arrow fly and was again accurate in her deadly aim bringing down the second warrior on her side of the charging line of attackers.

As Shield rose from his concealment opposite of Waters, he drew his sight on the nearest warrior and let fly his shaft to find its mark. The arrow sunk deep into the hip of the buckskin clad Crow causing him to drop to the neck of his mount. Holding tight to the mane, he searched for any protection nearby. Finding none, he followed the others down the trail and dropped over the riverbank to the sandbar. Shield fought his way through the thick willows and tall grasses to the false campsite, knowing Jeremiah would be outnumbered and in need of his help. Waters, sucking deep breaths of fear and concern, left her position by the rocks and ran to the aid of Jeremiah.

Although the shot from his rifle had dropped an attacker, the smoke cloud and loud report betrayed his position to the still charging leader. Jeremiah watched the warrior coax and kick his mount in an attempt to get the horse to penetrate the willows and climb the soft soil bank, but the horse fell to his knees in the vain attempt to climb. As he struggled to find footing, the warrior threw his leg over the mounts neck and dropped to his feet behind the small grove of Cottonwood between him and the white man. Choosing his pistol and his Green River knife instead of the readied bow, Jeremiah braced himself for the charge of the screaming Crow leader. Jeremiah's eyes widened as the Crow stepped from behind the Cottonwood. Jeremiah had not realized what a massive man

the warrior was and the upraised warclub made him appear
even larger. Although his hair flowed down his shoulders, the
feathers stood higher giving the appearance of greater height.
The bone and bead chest plate enhanced the thought of
invincibility, and the arm bands brought attention to the
bulging muscles in his upper arms and shoulders. His first look
of appraisal told Jeremiah this was a formidable foe. Without
hesitation, he raised his pistol hip high, leveled it at the now
charging and screaming Crow, pulled the trigger and was
startled at the result being nothing but the click of the dropping
hammer, misfire! Ducking under the expected blow, Jeremiah
drove his shoulder into the chest of the massive leader driving
him back against the rough bark of the towering cottonwood
and drove the blade of his knife between the left side ribs. The
warrior acted as if he had not felt the piercing of the blade and
hammered down on Jeremiah's back with the flat of the war
club. Jeremiah knew the club, twice the length of his arm and
as big as his leg, with a broad metal blade imbedded in the large
head, would certainly bring death if he didn't do something and
do it fast. He quickly stabbed at his attacker's side twice more,
then reaching down and behind the monsters legs he tried to
upset his opponent. Both bodies were slick with sweat and
blood and the stench of battle. White Wolf tried to draw on any
reserve power from the teaching of Black Kettle, Ezekiel and
his God. But because of the size and strength of the would-be
assailant, Jeremiah was unable to pull him down. The big
Indian had braced himself against the trunk of the tree and with
the bellow of an enraged bull bison, he began to force Jeremiah
back to give room for a death blow with the blade of the
warclub. With blood now smeared over his hand and knife
Jeremiah's grip was unsure, grasping the Indian's legs and with
another desperate swipe he severed the tendons behind the
assailant's knee. Losing his leverage, the Crow warrior
stumbled back against the tree, then leaning to the downhill
side grabbed at the wound to his leg.

With the release of the grip of the big Indian, Jeremiah dropped to his side and rolled away from the reach of the Crow leader. Within a second of his roll, he heard the whisper of an arrow, then another. The two shafts came from two directions and were deeply planted in the chest of the leader having pierced the decorative but useless chest plate. The Crow looked at the arrows protruding from his body and lifted his head as if to ask the question, why? No other sound came from him as he slowly crumpled to his side and rolled to his stomach then tumbled down the embankment breaking off the shafts and covering his body with the loose soil. From the height of the river bank and overlooking the now still body, they heard the death rattle escape from his lips.

"What about the others?" queried Jeremiah as he looked at Shield and Waters now standing by him.

"Dead or gone. Waters downed two, I put an arrow in one but the other one turned and fled after the wounded one. I think they will not return," replied Shield.

"I am glad I was here to protect you two brave warriors. Maybe I will go collect my scalps while you two fix a meal for us," chuckled Waters as she turned away.

Laughing Waters had never felt herself inferior to or better than either of the men. It had not been a subject of consideration in her culture, each person stands on their own merits. Although it was not common for a woman to follow the warrior path, it was a respected decision when made and more so when made by one of high status as Waters, the daughter of a highly respected tribal leader, Black Kettle. As Waters had proved herself the equal of any warrior and more skilled than most, her status had continually increased. However, now as her feelings for Jeremiah had changed, the choosing of a mate or being chosen as a mate became more complicated and her spirit was conflicted. Jeremiah gave her much joy when he looked at her and more so when they touched, emotions she had never experienced were now invading her once peaceful spirit. The question of her future path now troubled her.

As he watched Waters walk away, Jeremiah admired her confident stride and what seemed to be a bounce in her step that echoed the laughter she had left them with. "Brother, I don't think we will ever live this down," observed Jeremiah as he raised up and headed toward the camp and the waiting duties.

To Keep a Promise

Chapter Thirteen: Bounty

THE GIGGLE AND CHUCKLE of the river as it cascaded over the exposed boulders and rocks that created the rapids betrayed the low water level caused by the early winter season. With no snow melt in the mountains, the now frozen springs, and no storm brought moisture, the river presented few hazards to a low water crossing. The pristine water gave clear visibility to the river donies, the myriad of stones that littered the bottom of the stream and had been tumbled in the current giving them rounded and smooth shapes. That same clarity revealed an occasional rainbow trout peeking out from his hidey-hole of the overhanging bank as he waited for lunch in the form of any bug or worm unlucky enough to fall within his reach.

The clatter of the horses' hooves chased the trout into the dark recesses of his hole. The crossing of the small caravan muddied the waters as the river donies rolled in protest at the disturbance. The remaining three of the disreputable bunch of renegades waded the river in single file behind Frenchy DuBois. Dirty and disheveled and unkempt in their appearance, their looks were disgusting by any standard. Before leaving the stream, Frenchy leaned to his left and spat a gob of tobacco into the water and carelessly wiped at his now whiskered chin. It was evident that his wiping was not always successful as it appeared as much tobacco remained in his whiskers as he successfully expectorated. Turning back to his followers, he said, "Now you 'member what I said. You let me do all the talkin' ya hear?" Not expecting any response, he turned to rein his horse up the riverbank.

From the opposite bank, the renegades had spotted the activity of many men involved in some construction. The level site was in a sizable clearing away from any timber and near the river bank close to what could easily be made into a landing for small boats or rafts. The construction crew appeared to be erecting some walls of upright timbers in what the observers speculated might become some type of fort structure. With no uniforms in sight, Frenchy concluded it was probably going to be a trading fort to initiate trade with the various tribes in the area. This location was on the North edge of Crow territory, the South end of Blackfoot country, and not too far from some of the roaming Sioux bands. Frenchy told his men, "This might be a good place to trade those pelts we got from that big slave, Ezekiel." He also thought they could rid themselves of the three extra packhorses that were carrying the pelts and maybe convert some of the gold dust to coin. His men knew he found some gold, but he had refused to let them know how much. He had said it was just a couple of pouches and he would share it with them.

Driving his heels into the grey's ribs, DuBois reined his mount up the bank and through the sparse willows. Following close behind were the kid, Emity Chase, on his skinny sorrel mare and Almon Rosencrantz, the big whiner on his equally big bay gelding. The kid, Rosencrantz, and the renegade Arapaho, Walks-in-Water, each led a pack horse loaded with the bales of pelts stolen from Ezekiel and Jeremiah and carrying the small packs of their now diminished supplies.

They made their way to the construction site, passing two previously unseen cabins nestled against the scattered cottonwoods and willows on the riverbank. Frenchy noted the lean-tos at the ends of the cabins were piled with crates and panniers of supplies for the trading fort. Whenever he saw anything that held value, Frenchy would try to calculate how he could gain possession by any devious means, and his mind began to swirl with random ideas to gain more plunder. Nearing the building crew, he had to change his thinking and his expression as he called out, "Hello the camp!"

The nearest workers, some in buckskins and others in corded trousers held up by suspenders over the bloused sleeve shirts, turned to the newcomers and shouted a greeting in return. "Step on down, strangers, and welcome. I see you got yourselves a few pelts there. They from last winter?" said a tall, broad-shouldered, and red-bearded man with red cheeks and sporting a set of weathered and soiled buckskins. "I'm Samuel Tulloch, and I'm the bourgeois here at Fort Van Buren. Are ya lookin' to do some tradin'?"

"I'm Jean DuBois, most call me Frenchy, and yes, we want to do some tradin'. Gettin' a little low on some supplies and need to stock up a little 'fore we head up North. Looks like your just gettin' a good start on this here fort. Was this all your idea?"

"No, no, we're with the American Fur Company and this is just one of the new outposts. Ya say you're headin' North? That's Blackfoot country, you been there before?" asked Tulloch.

"Naw, we're not goin' to be doin' any trappin'. We heard that we could catch a boat from up there at Fort Union. We want to head back to civilization!"

Tulloch's first impression of Frenchy and crew was that of a bunch of raiders and renegades, not someone that wanted anything to do with cities and civilization except for more opportunities to steal and destroy. With a nod of his head, several of his men casually strolled around the horses and men as if to look at the bales of pelts in anticipation of a trade. Although they had been working at building the fort, each man was armed with a pistol in his belt and a knife in a scabbard at his side. Realizing they were outnumbered and he wasn't dealing with an easily deceived trader, Frenchy quickly decided to make his trade and move along. Stepping down from his mount, he continued his conversation with the bourgeois.

"Say, I noticed you had some canoes and rafts tied up down below. Did you fellas come upstream from Union?"

"Yeah, we brought most of our gear up mid-summer when the water was a little higher. Couldn't do it now, wouldn't be enough clearance for a heavy loaded boat," replied Tulloch.

While the conversation continued and the trading began, the rest of Frenchy's crew sought a bit of shade to stretch their legs and subtly observe the activity of the construction on the fort. Frenchy followed Tulloch as he walked around the pelt laden horses examining the furs.   "So, you think we might make it down river to Ft. Union?" queried Frenchy.

"Well, now, I guess that all depends," replied Tulloch.

"Depends? Depends on what?"

"On whether or not you got a boat. If you know anything about rivers. On how much of a load you be carryin' and how soon you wanna get there," observed Tulloch.

"Well, we ain't got no boat, don't know nuthin' 'bout rivers, and ain't carryin' much of a load. Say, you think we might trade for a couple of your canoes?" questioned Frenchy.

"Then it sounds to me like you're up a crik without a . . . "

"Yeah, I know, without a paddle. But, I notice you ain't got many horses here and it looks to me like you sure could use some. Draggin' those timbers down, and goin' huntin' for meat and all. If we could get a couple of boats, we'd trade these here horses," responded Frenchy with a grin. He was sure he had hit on a solution to his plan. He was anxious to get this bounty hunting trip over and get back to Kentucky. Even though Kentucky wasn't the center of civilization, at least there were houses and beds, and he was tired of sleeping on the ground. Since stealing the parfleche of gold pouches from that slave, Ezekiel, he had begun to dream a bit bigger than usual. Now he had designs of buying a big house and filling it up with women, the kind of women who wouldn't look at him now, but sure change their tune when they smell money.

Tulloch stepped around from behind the last packhorse and eyeing Frenchy, he responded, "We need our boats. We have to take the pelts and stuff to Ft. Union in the Spring to ship to St. Louis and we need to bring the foo feraw and other supplies back up stream."

"Hmm . . .what about hirin' out a couple of your men to take us to Ft. Union and then they can bring the boats back. That way we're both happy," suggested DuBois. When he saw something he wanted, he was like a rabid badger, sinking his teeth in and refusing to let go. He was determined to work his will on this man. Who was he to try to stop Frenchy?

"I need all my men for getting' this post built."

"Yeah, but having more horses to snake those timbers down here will get more done than any two men. Besides, I noticed a couple of your workers don't seem to be workin' real hard. How 'bout sendin' those two coloreds with us and they can bring the boats back before you even miss 'em," proposed Frenchy.

Sensing the weakening of the bourgeois, Frenchy sought to close the deal. "I tell you what I'll do. You let those boys take us down, and I'll give you an extra $100 in gold dust. Just to make sure you're happy with the deal and you've got something to show for it."

The bourgeois put one arm over the neck of the pack horse and turned to face the stubborn Frenchman. He had some reservations, but they did need the horses and an extra bit of gold dust in his pocket wouldn't be bad either. It would take a couple of weeks wading in icy waters an' pulling up beaver to equal what he could make with just a nod of his head.

The grey light of early morning was slowly peeking above the Eastern horizon as the two canoes with three men each, were pushed away sucking their bows from the muddy bank at the junction of the Tongue and Yellowstone rivers. The lead boat held the kid in the bow, Rosencrantz in the center surrounded by most of the gear and the rented black man, Rufus, in the stern. The fat man, Rosencrantz, had all he could do to steady himself and not upset the canoe, while the kid was enjoying the view from the front. The kid had never been in a boat of any kind before but he took to it handily, he reveled at the power of the deep and long strokes as he pulled the canoe into the small waves of the river. Under the direction of the big black man, the kid deftly handled his task and quickly learned the need of taking the rapids in the center and straight on with the bow of the canoe. He also realized the man in the stern was the one that had the real control of the craft.

Rufus was a freed slave from Philadelphia and had anxiously answered the call put out by the American Fur Company for willing workers and trappers to go to the frontier. Because he didn't have the money to outfit himself, he was hired on as a worker to do the menial chores and work the trappers shirked. He met up with Jake, the other negro on this venture, when the boats were loading in St. Louis. Jake was a runaway but no one knew that but Rufus. The bigger of the two and the more brash of manner, Rufus took on the role of big brother to Jake. The younger man was smaller than Rufus' 6 foot, but only by about 3 inches and 30 pounds. While Rufus was broad shouldered, deep chested and had a narrow waist and deep black color, Jake appeared lean and downcast although he was agile, stronger than he appeared, and quick-of-mind.

Jake was in the captain's seat in the stern of the second boat, maneuvering the craft easily among the scattered boulders and small rapids. Frenchy knelt in the bow of the boat and sporadically dipped his paddle in the swift flowing waters, just enough to appear as if he were helping. He focused on the river ahead and calculated the next steps of his plan to gain more bounty and reach their destination without any more delay. The Indian, in the middle of the canoe amidst the gear, was on his knees and readily used the provided paddle. It was obvious that he was experienced with handling a canoe like the birchbark craft they now occupied.

The two canoes quietly slipped through the waters leaving no evidence of their passing while the passengers took in the limited views of the crowded riverbanks. When the river curved, the opposing bank was crowded with Ash and Boxelder with occasional clumps of choke cherry bushes, and when the river sought a straighter course, the low lying banks held nothing but wild grasses like foxtail and fescue that would wave to the passing wanderers. Walks-in-Water, true to his Indian way, had been watchful for any wild game that might come down the riverbank for water or to graze on the greener grasses near the flowing stream. As the canoes maneuvered the bend of the river, two mule deer, a doe and a small buck, were startled and froze in their stare of the strange objects on the stream. Frenchy turned and dug for his flintlock under their gear, but Walks-in-Water had already drawn his bow and loosed an arrow to fetch their dinner. The larger of the two deer turned to mount the riverbank and escape but her steps faltered as she fell while the smaller buck jumped her carcass in a spring-loaded hop and disappeared over the edge of the grassy bank.

Not more than thirty yards downstream from where Walks-in-Water was butchering his kill, a cottonwood and willow covered shoulder of land jutted into the river and Frenchy made the decision to camp for the night. It was nearing sundown as the five men unloaded the canoes of their bedrolls and gear needed to make camp. The campsite had been used before by both man and animals as evidenced by a fire circle and matted down grasses for beds. It was not unusual for deer and bear to bed down in protected areas such as this, as long as the previous occupants were not recent visitors.

With little conversation but an occasional grunt or directive from Frenchy, the camp quickly took shape, a fire started, and the meal prepared. After Walks returned with the deer carcass, he cut several strips of meat, placed them on fresh cut willow branches that overhung the fire, and awaited the sizzle of the slow cooking meat. Rosencrantz had hung a pot of beans from a tripod over the fire and the kid was busy preparing some pan bread. They had replenished their supply of coffee, flour, sugar and beans at the Fort, but were unable to trade for any meat. The fresh venison was eagerly anticipated by everyone as they seated themselves around the fire and poured cups of fresh brewed strong coffee.

Rufus and Jake were the first ones to turn in as they had done most of the work paddling the canoes on this first day's trip down the Yellowstone. They made their beds near one another on the upstream side of the camp and near the taller of the cottonwoods. The other four were opposite the campfire with Frenchy, a bit farther away and near the bunch of chokecherry bushes on the downstream side of the camp. Not seeing a need for posting a guard, within a short time all the travelers slept. The normal night harmonies of owls, night birds, and rodents were disturbed by the coughs and snores of the men, with the snuffle and snore of Rufus exceeding them all.

Frenchy's feigned slumber turned to wide-eyed wakefulness as he rolled to his side and with slitted eyes surveyed the still forms of the camp. With a stealth that belied his deformed stature, he disappeared into the trees away from the glowing coals of the fire. He stepped carefully as the built-up sole of his boot was now more an enemy than an aid, making it impossible to feel any stone or twig beneath his foot, that if stirred or broken, would betray his presence. He slowly approached the large cottonwoods, felt their rough bark, and stilled his breathing. He slipped the .40 caliber flintlock pistol from his waistband, felt the pan and hammer to be sure all was set, then pulled his knife from the scabbard on his hip.

With a snort and a cough, Rufus rolled to his back and returned to his sawmill snoring. Jake was within an arms length with his back to his friend and the rhythmic rise of his arm on his side told of a deep sleep. The movement of Rufus startled

Frenchy causing him to step behind the grey barked tree but he now stepped to the side to launch his attack. As his lip curled in a snarl, two steps brought him beside the big black man, then cocking his leg back with the swing of a sledge, he let fly his boot to the side of Rufus head. Catching his skull at the temple with the weighted boot, blood spurted into Rufus thick hair and over his face while he emitted a blood-smothered gurgle, and Frenchy lowered his pistol and aligned it to the back of Jake. The smaller of the two black men rolled to the sound of his friend and the whites of his eyes were illumined with the reflected glow of the fire. His legs were tangled in his blankets as he thrashed to escape, but the .40 caliber ball pierced his breast bone and forced the negro to his back into the quickly spreading blood pool and mussed blankets.

Frenchy dropped to one knee beside the still form of Rufus and with the oft-practiced move, slit the black throat from ear to ear, letting escape the choked down blood from the dead man's neck. Frenchy gained the side of Jake's inert body and repeated his action on the escaped slave. Rising to stand over his victims, Frenchy turned to see his companions staring across the fire at the bloody assassin. "Whatchu lookin' at? You know we ain't gonna share our gold with these two worthless pieces of trash!"

A weak reply squeaked from the kid, "I thot we needed 'em to git downriver. You know, over dem rapids an such."

"We don't need nobody 'er nuttin'" retorted Frenchy as he dropped to one knee between the two bodies. With four sawing strokes, he liberated all four ears from the two black victims. He sat back on his heels and admired his handiwork, but his scrutiny of his trophies was interrupted by another query from the campfire.

"Did you cut off their ears? Whatcha wanna do that fer?" asked the kid.

With a furious and terse reply, Frechy shouted, "Fer bounty, you fool. We get $200 bounty for every pair of slaves ears we bring back!"

Chapter Fourteen: Honor

THE LONG SHADOWS of dusk were erased by the deeper darkness of night as a distant single wolf hung his lonesome howl on the last quarter of the moon. The diamond tidbits on the black velvet night whispered the secrets of heaven to the numb minds of the slumbering vengeance seekers. It had been a tiring and battle scarred day and the deep-seated memories again badgered the sleep deprived Jeremiah. Seldom did he enjoy a full night's undisturbed rest, with so many unanswered questions regarding the many momentous events of his young life. He couldn't remember how many nights he had startled himself awake with the realistic dreams of loved ones slain. And always the question, why? Why did they have to die? Why couldn't he help them? Ezekiel had said those were questions that a boy shouldn't be asking and that maybe when he became a man he might find the answers. *Become a man? I'm full-growed now, I've killed men in battle, ain't I a man now? But I still don't have the answers. And Laughing-Waters, she sure makes me feel like a man. Oh, shut-up, close your eyes and get some sleep, we got travelin' to do!*

Two days of uneventful travel brought the three within view of the construction still underway at Fort VanBuren. It was an unexpected sight and the travelers dropped back below the slight rise to be unseen by the fort's occupants.

"What is it that they do? So many white men working there?" inquired Shield of Jeremiah.

"Well, from what I could tell, it looks like they're building a fort of some kind. Probably for tradin' cuz I didn't see sojers there, you know, no uniforms and such," replied Jeremiah.

"Should we go in to trade? Or mebbe go 'round?" mused Shield.

"Well, we got a couple extra horses, and we could use some more coffee. Let's go down and see what we can do. Maybe we can find out somethin' about those renegades, too," answered Jeremiah.

The smile on Laughing Waters face showed her agreement as she leaned into the lead rope of her pack-horse. They followed the path of the renegades to the river crossing and approached the hectic activity of the fort's workers. Two men had shouldered a sizable timber and were carrying their load to the newly turned sod in line with the partially erected wall of timbers. Three others were digging a trough that evidently was for the placement of the uprights for the perimeter. Still others were leaning on ladders on the inside of the already erected river-side wall to secure a walkway to the uprights. On the uphill side of the timber, one man was driving a harnessed horse and pulling a newly felled tree into the open. Two more were trimming previously felled logs of branches and excess bark, making them ready for use as an upright. Several more were busy carrying tools or wood and scurried about with purpose.

With a loud, "Hello, the camp!" the travelers made their way to the clearing beside the construction. A burly bearded man with the look of a timberjack, shouted back, "Hallooo." With dirtied suspenders stretching over brawny shoulders and frayed red union suit, trousers of dark wool, and high top lace up boots, the stocking capped man strode nearer the mounted trio. Jeremiah thought to himself that if anyone ever resembled a whiskey barrel in size and girth, this man surely did. Jeremiah stepped down from his appaloosa and wrapped the lead rope of the pack horse around the saddle horn.

"So'd ya come to do some tradin' are ya?" asked the whiskey barrel.

"Well, mebbe so, we could use some supplies," responded Jeremiah, as he looked about the busy site.

The barrel turned and shouted over his shoulder, "Hey, git that boosh way over here. These here folk goin' do some tradin'!" Turning back to Jeremiah, he said, "Whatcha goin' trade? Sure'n I don't see no pelts, ye be bringin' or are ya tradin' the favors of that wee lass back there?"

Jeremiah looked at the boisterous man, then to Laughing Waters, and realizing what the man was implying, he firmly said, "No! But we've got a couple hides and some spare horses some raiding Crow donated that we are willing to part with."

Samuel Tulloch, the bourgeois, arrived at the group in time to hear this exchange and said to the barrel, "That'll be enough of that, MacGregor, now get back to work." With a grumble that barely escaped his beard, the man turned to his assigned task. Tulloch spoke to Jeremiah, "So, you're looking to do some tradin' are ya? I'm Samuel Tulloch, what is it you're needing and what are you trading?"

Liking the look of the blond bearded man, Jeremiah responded with a smile and an extended hand, "I'm Jeremiah Thompsett, these are my friends, Broken Shield and Laughing Waters. We are looking to shed a couple of these pack horses and a couple of deer hides for some staples, and maybe a little powder and lead."

"Fine, fine. Won't you step over here to the cabin, and we'll see if we can't fix you up with what you need. You all travelin' very far?" queried Tulloch.

"Well, that kinda depends. We're on the trail of some murderin' renegades and their trail indicates they passed through here. Three white men and a renegade Arapaho. Have you had some visitors lately?" asked Jeremiah. The bourgeois

111

was leading the trio to the larger of the two cabins and paused before entering the rough-hewn door.

"Sounds like a bunch that was through here a couple o' days ago. The white men, one squirrely looking with a limp, a fat sloppy one and a mean lookin' kid?" asked Tulloch.

"That's them. They murdered my partner, burnt our cabin, stole our furs and some gold, and lit out. We've been after 'em for better'n two weeks. They left three behind to ambush us, but we took care of them. These are their horses we want to trade."

"Well, you're only a couple of days behind them. What you say doesn't surprise me. I didn't like the looks of them when they were here. But, I traded them the use of a couple of canoes and they set out with a couple of my men two days ago. You'll have a hard time catchin' them overland cuz they can make better time on the water."

Slamming his fist into his open palm, Jeremiah exclaimed, "Just when we get close, too. What did you mean 'the use of a couple of canoes'?"

Tulloch replied, "Well, I sent two of my men with them to bring the canoes back after they get to Ft. Union."

Jeremiah's expression revealed his alarm, and dropping his head, he said quietly, "I don't think you'll ever see those canoes again, or the men, for that matter. Who were the men?"

"Well, they weren't trappers, but they were pretty good workers, for ex-slaves," replied Tulloch.

Jeremiah's head snapped up, "Ex-slaves? Well that tears it. I'm sure you won't see them again then. I'm thinkin' that bunch was slave-hunters."

As they concluded their haggling and bickering over the trades, Tulloch suggested, "Since it's gittin' on dark, if you wanna spend the night, you can tether your horses in the clearing and pitch your bedrolls on the downhill side of the cabins. There's a pretty good spot just below the bank drop off. Others have camped there as you can tell by the fire makin's."

"We'll probably do that, our horses could use a good feed on that good gramma grass in the clearing. We won't tether 'em, we'll just hobble 'em. They should be fine. Thanks for the offer. We'll be headin' out before light in the mornin' so we'll pack our stuff up tonite," commented Jeremiah.

"Ya know, if ya 'all wanna save a little time. There's no trail, but if you shy away from follerin' the river, bear straight North East, you'll hit the Missouri and foller it downriver to the Fort, ya might save a day or two," offered Tulloch. "I trapped up in that country a couple years ago, and it would be easier and faster travelin' thata way. "

Jeremiah responded with a, "Thanks, I 'preciate it. We'd like to catch 'em 'fore they git a boat away from there."

With a nod of his head, the bourgeois turned back to the fort to make use of the last bit of daylight. The trio of travelers led their horses down the slight slope to the designated camp site and unloaded the packs. After rubbing down the horses, Shield led them to the clearing to secure their hobbles and let them graze. Waters and Jeremiah teamed up to get the fire started and start the meal, each busy about their tasks with little need for conversation. Jeremiah would sneak a look at the graceful and simply attired Waters, with each look stirring up his emotions. His gaze lingered on her buckskin dress, noting the simple decorative beading that enhanced the womanly chest and the buckskin hugging her curves. His observation did not go unnoticed by Waters. She turned to look at him, striking a bold stance with feet spread slightly apart, one hand on a hip and the opposite one cocked to the side, accenting the swell of her curves and the smallness of her waist. "Are you just going to watch me, or are you going to help?" she said with a mischievous smile, knowing the effect she had on him was not that different than his effect on her.

Stammering and stumbling to pick up a piece of firewood, Jeremiah said, "Uh, yeah, I'm helpin', see, I'm gettin' the wood."

"Yeah, sonny boy. Yo be gittin' the firewood, and let a real man take care of this woman," came a rumbling voice from the grove of willows. Stepping out on the sandy bank, the whiskey barrel named MacGregor, bared his teeth from behind the tobacco darkened beard and leered at the startled pair.

"What are you doin' here? What do you want?" called Jeremiah, as he made his way to stand between Waters and the intruder. The only weapon within reach was the Green River knife still in the scabbard sitting on Jeremiah's hip. He slowly dropped his hand to grip the handle, wishing he had his pistol instead.

The movement was observed by MacGregor and he said, "Sonny, that there knife wouldna be doin' ya any good. I'm a master at the rough and tumble fightin' and a mere little blade like that won't help atall. Just you be steppin' aside, and I'll be done in a little while. Never you mind, now, yahear?"

Jeremiah slid one foot to the side to broaden his stance. He would not give way to this man. Although Jeremiah was taller, it was evident that MacGregor was broader and undoubtedly more experienced. As the intruder neared Jeremiah, he smirked and laughed in an attempt to relax his mark. With a slight crouch, Jeremiah brought his fist from the handle of the knife, swooping near the ground and up under MacGregor's chin, laying the Scotsman on his back. Rolling to his side, and spitting blood, the barrel of a man brought his knees under him and jumped to his feet. "Well, me bucko, you pack a pretty good wallop there. But it won't be doin' ya any good," he said as he lowered his shoulders and charged at the mountain man.

Taking the shoulder in his gut, Jeremiah lost his breath and the barrel of a man drove him to the ground. Gasping for air, Jeremiah felt like he had a boulder on his chest and he couldn't get wind. The now enraged beast straddled Jeremiah's legs and began to pound each side of his head in opposing blows from his hammer like fists. Jeremiah was numbed to the blows as a blackness began to close in around him. Spitting blood and pushing with all his strength, he felt relief and sucked for some air. As MacGregor rose from the now prostrate form of the mountain man, he kicked Jeremiah in the side and heard the crack of ribs. "That'll teach ya to mess with me, sonny boy," he muttered as he raised his heavy boot to smash down on his victim's face. The upraised leg stopped in mid-swing as the Scotsman staggered back a step. Looking down at the feathers protruding from his thigh, he said, "What th . . . what is this?" As he looked at Laughing Waters holding her bow with another arrow notched in the string and aimed at him, "Why you crazy squaw. You shot me! You coulda killed me!"

"I could have. But I chose not to, but this next one is aimed just a little bit higher. If you don't leave, the last thing you will feel is these feathers passing through your fat belly. So, please, stay and let me do that for you, white man," said a sober faced Laughing Waters.

"I'll fix you, you crazy squaw. Wait'll I get my men. I'll be back," he threatened over his shoulder as he limped away. Broken Shield returned leading the horses, explained to Waters that he had seen what happened and knew they would need to leave. He helped Jeremiah to his feet and the two men quickly saddled and packed the horses and within minutes the trio was again crossing the river to make their escape.

Every step and sway of the horse beneath Jeremiah brought some form of grunt or complaint from the battered and humbled man. He had never been beaten like this, and it all happened so fast. The bull of a man was a formidable foe that had been underestimated by Jeremiah and it was a lesson learned and accented by the bruises and swelling to what Jeremiah thought was his entire body. But it was a matter of honor. That's what his father had taught him. *No matter the foe, when you are obliged to protect those you love, it is a matter of honor. You may get beat, but never yield your honor. That is the making of a man.* Jeremiah could remember his father speaking those words as clearly as if he stood before him now. Honor. Honor was worth fighting for, never yield your honor.

To Keep a Promise

Chapter Fifteen: Caught

IRREGULAR TERRAIN, rolling hills that gave way to rocky escarpments and flat plateaus, all were painted with the careless strokes of random juniper clusters with backgrounds of sagebrush, yucca, and cholla cactus and known as the plains against the Big Sheep Mountains. Some of the mountains were covered with pinion and juniper with an occasional cedar thrown in, but the rocky outcrops were as frequent as the ravines that scarred the hillsides with both looking like afterthoughts to the creator. Four short nights and four long days of travel by the rapidly tiring trio through this erratic and unpredictable country finally yielded the long sought destination. Cresting the rise of a smaller hill overlooking the confluence of the Yellowstone and Missouri rivers, the travelers allowed their eyes to linger on the imposing walls of Ft. Union.

This was the largest structure that Shield and Waters had ever seen. With a square shape made of upright peeled timbers all evenly trimmed to provide the four walls, two opposing corners held large blockhouses extending out from the walls to provide a line of sight and fire covering two walls each, with walkways at the top for defenders. The large two story structure inside the blockade was the residence of the bourgeois, while other structures within the walls housed the smithy, cooling shed, fur storage, armory, and bunkhouse for the workers and trappers. Both Shield and Waters were held speechless as they sought to take in the amazing site and activity surrounding the fort. There were several teepees in a small village arrangement North of the fort, and other temporary shelters erected in other groups to the East. A small herd of horses grazed lazily to the West on a grassy plain and were watched over by two men on horseback. Originally built by the American Fur Company at the request of the Assiniboine tribe to further their trade, Ft. Union was already known as the largest and most profitable trading post in the nation.

Standing up in his stirrups and to the East, Jeremiah surveyed the confluence of the Yellowstone with the mighty Missouri river. Knowing the renegades were traveling on the Yellowstone, he felt they would beach the canoes and camp near the confluence. "Let's go take a look down by the meeting of the rivers. I think we might find our prey somewhere thereabouts," he stated as he nudged his mount off the hilltop. He had been certain they were at the end of their quest and would soon confront the perpetrators they had sought for so long.

There was nothing but a scattering of grasses between them and the wooded riverbank as their horses continued their trail covering stride toward the cottonwoods that were now bare of any leaves. The skeleton forms of the trees clawed upward in a vain attempt to scratch the blue of the afternoon sky while the prairie breeze whipped the willows at their bases. Jeremiah dismounted, grabbed his rifle still in the fringed scabbard, and motioned to Shield to ground tie the horses and join him. Waters dropped silently to the ground, bow in hand, and slipped an arrow from the quiver at her waist. They walked stealthily yet boldly and maintained the tree line as cover between them and anyone on the grassy sand bank

118

below. The riverbank dropped steeply about five feet to the sand bar that was often used as a campsite by visitors to the fort. As anticipated, two canoes were beached and overturned side by side below a sparse campsite of a campfire and some bedrolls. Lounging lazily against a driftwood log was the Arapaho renegade with his feet to the fire while the kid approached with an armload of driftwood firewood.

Jeremiah dropped to one knee and bent to conceal himself behind the willows. Shield and Waters mimicked Jeremiah. "Just as I thought. Here they are," whispered Jeremiah to his companions.

"But where are the other two? There are three bedrolls, but only two are here." Observed Shield.

After a quick scan of the nearby cover, Jeremiah stated, "I think the other two are probably over at the fort. Maybe this is our chance to take these two first."

Shield had been closely observing the two, then turned to Waters, "Does that warrior look like someone you know?"

"That's Walks-in-water, he was put out of our camp when he refused the council's command about when he attacked me," responded Laughing Waters through her clenched teeth. It was evident by her expression that this was not a pleasant memory and it rankled her and brought tension to her stance.

Jeremiah watched as the two siblings talked, but upon hearing this he quickly turned and asked, "Attacked you? When? Why didn't I know about it? What happened?" His voice had risen and she shushed him with a hand motion to her mouth.

"It doesn't matter now. It was when you were gone hunting with Ezekiel two summers ago. He tried to force himself on me and Shield stopped him. Walks ran away, but the council knew what happened and he didn't make it right, so they put him out of the village," she responded just above a whisper trying to make it brief and not alarm the two below. But Shield had risen and dropped off the riverbank to stand before the two renegades, with an arrow strung in his bow and a look of steel in his eyes.

When Shield had dropped to the sandbar, the startled Walks-in-Water jumped to his feet and bent to reach his bow behind the log. "Stop!" yelled Shield. The renegade froze in his sideways motion and slowly raised himself upright, turning to face the intruder. The shout and subsequent movement had surprised the kid causing him to drop the firewood and turn towards Shield. Thinking to use the kid as a barrier to his movements, Walks tried to slowly move to his right. Again a shout from Shield stopped him. With his bow fully drawn now, Shield instructed the kid to move aside. Walks noted the other two pursuers drop from the riverbank to the sandbar. Bringing his eyes back to Shield, he said, "So, you come to me again. It has been a long time, my brother. And I see you brought the prize with you. Did you come to give her to me, like you should have before?" It was evident the renegade wanted to shake the confidence of his adversary, Shield.

With a stoic expression, Shield simply stated, "I have come to exact vengeance upon you, you worthless piece of skunk dung. This will be a better place when I send you to walk with your ancestors." Without taking his eyes from the renegade, Shield set his bow and quiver of arrows to the side, pulled his tomahawk from his waistband with his right hand, his knife from the scabbard at his hip with his left hand, and said, "Arm yourself."

With the grin of a wolverine eyeing its next meal, Walks bent to pick up his weapons. He turned back with a tomahawk in his left hand and a spear in his right. "Now we shall see who is the real warrior and when I finish you, I will enjoy my time with your sister," snarled the circling fighter. Shield knew he had to be wary, as it had often been said about Walks that he should have been named after coyote, because he was definitely a trickster. The two adversaries dropped to a slight crouch, arms outstretched with weapons, and began circling each other. Their movements were slightly hampered because of the loose sand of the site by the riverside. When the spring snowmelt had swollen the waters in the high country rivulets, the lower streams and rivers would often wash out their banks and leave behind piles of driftwood on the sandy riverside. This was where the renegades had chosen to camp and was now the site of the conflict between former childhood friends, as they began the dance of death in the sand.

Shield focused on the eyes of Walks, matching him step by step in the circular movement. Walks, wanting to intimidate his opponent, wrinkled his face into a snarl and emitted a low growl, and feinted with his spear. With the longer reach of the flint pointed lance, Walks thought he had the advantage, but Shield was the quicker and more agile of the two. Whenever Walks would thrust his spear seeking to pierce his opponent, Shield would adroitly step aside and counter the thrust with his hatchet. Shield noted that an instant before each move, Walks would slightly squint his eyes in anticipation of his action. Shield was biding his time and carefully noted each move, all the while maintaining his defensive posture. Each failed thrust with the spear further frustrated Walks and he became more aggressive, thinking Shield was showing fear and success would soon be his to claim.

Walks stopped, a low growl started deep in his chest, he let out a scream, dropped his knife and thrust the spear forward with both hands in a deadly grip. The sudden charge and scream startled the wary Shield, his sidestep hampered by the sand and the spear point laid open his side. The glancing blow sent pain rushing through his body, but he regained his footing and stepped back from the spear. Walks sought to give the finishing thrust and overstepped his reach as Shield brought his hatchet down on the shaft of the spear and shattered the lance shaft between the hands of Walks. Shield spun to the side and dug his knife across the side and back of Walks drawing blood from the lengthy gash. With the roar of a wounded bear, Walks dropped the broken shaft retaining the portion with the flint point, picked up his knife and pursued Shield toward the smoldering coals of the fire as Shield adroitly leaped the firepit. Shield turned to face Walks, as both regained the fighting crouch again circling the other, each now more wary of his adversary.

With his left side facing Shield, Walks flipped the spear point in his right hand, and with a half turn brought the broken lance overhead to throw at Shield successfully impaling the flint point in Shields left thigh causing him to drop to one knee. Seizing his opportunity, Walks charged the kneeling warrior and bowled him over with his attack. The two grappled with each other rolling down the sloping sand towards the water, blood smearing both bodies and each man gasping for breath and grabbing for an advantage. When the spear struck Shield in the thigh, he dropped his knife and extracted the spear point, casting it aside. Now Shield had only his steel bladed tomahawk and Walks was armed only with his knife in his right hand. As they struggled in the sand, Shield extended his right leg and stopped the roll with Shield astraddle the bleeding Walks, but the renegade sought to drive his knife into his opponent's side and had it deflected by the bloody hand of Shield. As Shield pushed the knife away, he drew back his hawk with his right hand and brought it down with the death blow that buried the metal blade in the forehead of the exiled Walks-in-Water. The exhausted Shield rolled to the side onto his back and gasped for air.

Jeremiah, Laughing Waters, and the kid were all mesmerized observers of the bloody battle and had maintained their distance from the bout. Jeremiah now stepped to his prostrate friend on the sandy riverside, but a muffled cry turned his attention back to Waters. She had been grabbed from behind by the kid who now held her with a hand over her mouth and a knife at her throat. "Now, you two just stay where you are. Me and this little lady are gonna be gittin' outa here. So don't you go tryin' nuthin', ya hear? Now, where's yore horses?" asked the kid.

Before Jeremiah could respond, an explosion of thunder and smoke came from atop the riverbank above them. The .54 caliber ball that hurtled from the white cloud wasted no time on its way to explode the side of the kid's head and dropped him dead to the ground. Jeremiah and Shield both took a defensive stance as Jeremiah brought his rifle to his shoulder and Shield searched for his bow and quiver. Before Jeremiah could draw a bead, he was surprised by a sound that mimicked the cackle of a sage hen and emanated from behind the few willows at the base of a twisted cottonwood. "Hee hee heeee," came a giggle from the bush. "Now hold on there young un', don't go doin' sumpin' with that there smokepole that you and me both will be regrettin'. " A twisted and somewhat comedic figure slowly rose from the ground and with a gait that was more of a waddle, he made his way to the edge of the riverbank, and in an imitation of a river otter, slid down to land on his feet before the surprised trio. Attired in well-used buckskins, with a powder horn and possibles bag over one shoulder and casually holding a flintlock rifle that appeared to be longer than he was tall, with brown and silver whiskers and hair sticking out in every direction, something resembling a porcupine stood gazing at the three very amazed travelers.

With another cackle and a squeal that brought images of an irritated lynx, the bundle of perplexity spoke, "Well, little lady, you all right? I didn't mean ta scare ya like that, but it seemed like the only thing to do. That piss ant looked like he was wantin' to slit your throat clear to next week." If it was possible for the entire frontier and every animal it held to be tied up in one small package, the man that stood before them certainly did that. As he looked at their bewildered expressions, open mouths, and unmoving postures, he said, "I'm Scratch. Leastwise that's what them that knows me calls me. And if there's food on, I most always answer. So, whatcha young un's up to, anyhow?"

Shaking his head and looking askance at the mountain man standing before them, Jeremiah managed to utter, "Where did you come from?"

"Why, right yonder. Didn'tcha see me over there?"

"O.K., but why were you there in the first place?" queried Jeremiah.

"Well, ya see, it's like this. I was over at the Sutler's havin' me a whiskey, and these two fellers were talkin' at a table next to the winder. Course, since I got such good listenin', I heerd 'em talkin' 'bout these two fellers over here and how they was wantin' to git rid of 'em. But then the squirrely lookin' one told the fat one to wait there and he'd be back. But he took off and left on that steamboat thingy without the fat one knowin' it. When fat boy found out he set out to wailin' like a stuck pig and tried to drown himself in that likker. So, bein' the curious sort, I thot I'd just see what these two were up to, and lo and behold, I durn near stepped into an injun war! That's when I just had to up and help this purty little thing. So, what else ya think ya need to know?"

"The squirrely lookin' one that left, did he have a game leg and a boot with the soles all built up like?" asked Jeremiah.

"Yup, that's the one. He took off packin' two or three parfleches and saddlebags, and he shore acted like he was in a hurry. He just did make that boat leavin'"

As the two men were conversing, Waters made her way to the side of her brother and began tending his wounds. He had lost quite a bit of blood and was struggling with the pain, but Waters' skills were evident as she cleaned and bound first his side, then the thigh and two other lesser wounds on his torso. Shield was now sitting on the log by the firepit as Waters continued ministering to his wounds.

Jeremiah asked Scratch, "Is the fat one still at the fort?"

"I think so. Hard tellin' 'bout some folks tho. He looked like he was as outta place as a sunbonnet on an Injun. Why?"

"We've been after them for a couple of weeks now. They killed my partner and robbed us. I gotta talk to that one and see if he can tell me anything about the one that took the boat."

"Well, why don't we just skedaddle over yonder and take care o' that?"

To Keep a Promise

Chapter Sixteen: River

AS JEREMIAH PUSHED the birchbark canoe away from the sandy bank, he deftly stepped into the bow and settled into a comfortable position on his knees, picked up the carved paddle and turned his face downstream. This was not his first choice of travel as he had never been comfortable around water and especially not in a frail craft like the canoe. From his childhood, Jeremiah had never lived near any significant bodies of water or rivers and without the experience nor opportunity to learn how to swim, he just didn't feel very safe as the canoe seemed to waddle like a duck with every move of his paddle. Scratch was an experienced river traveler and chose to take the position in the stern that would give him better control of the craft. As the duo settled into the movement of the river and were making good headway, Jeremiah began to relax and do his part. "So, Jeremiah, I seen you was strugglin' a little when you was sayin' yore goodbyes to that little filly. You kinda sweet on her, are ya?" asked Scratch.

"Well, all three of us have kinda growed up together. We ain't never been too far apart for any length of time," replied the younger man. That can't see anything and staring at something look painted his face as he remembered the goodbyes with his friends. Waters told him to take care of himself and hurry back home because she would be waiting. He stood silently with his hands at her waist as he searched for the right words that never came.

"Now, that there ain't what I asked ya. It was as plain to me as a sunrise o'er the snowy mountains, yore in love with that gal," observed the old-timer, his gravel voice bringing Jeremiah back to the present. "After you git done with this hyar doin's, yore gonna come back to her ain'tcha?"

"Well, I'd like to, but I'm thinkin' it's goin' to be some time before I get back here and she might not be into waitin' for me," replied Jeremiah.

"Aw shucks, son, if she loves ya, she'll wait. An' if she don't wait, ya don't wan her anyways. It were the best thing for them two to head on back home cuz where we're goin' there ain't too many folks that are very friendly to any injuns. I knowed of some purty bad things that folks have done to 'em and vicey versey too."

"Well, we've got a long ways to go. By the way, just why did you want to come along anyway?" asked Jeremiah.

"I told ya onct. Cuz, where yur a goin' is where I'm from and it's been a long time since I been ta home. Ya know what that is don'tcha? That place where ya growed up. So, you got some other reason for chasin' after this feller, other what he stole from ya?"

"Well, it has to do with a promise I made. My daddy said that the measure of a man is how well he keeps his word. And a promise is giving your word to someone that you'll do what you say. So, I guess to measure up, I'm gonna do my best to keep that promise."

This was the best time to be traveling on the river. Although the water level was a little high due to the late rains and early wet snows in the mountains, it was still low and smooth yet swift enough to make the light craft move easily and the travelers make good time.   As dusk set in, the duo looked for a spot on the bank to make camp and fix some supper. The grassy banks and sparse trees offered many easy to reach places providing both shelter and cover. They decided on a site, beached the canoe, made camp and started the fire and supper. When they sat by the fire and finished their meal, the conversation picked up again.

"So, can I ask ya 'bout that there promise that's makin' ya travel half way cross the known world just to keep it?" inquired the grizzled trapper.

After examining the face of his new companion, Jeremiah dropped his eyes to the fire and began telling the story of his being saved by Ezekiel and his youth with him and the Arapaho people. Omitting many of the details and ending his story with the promise to help Ezekiel free his family from slavery, Jeremiah summarized with, ". . . so, since they killed Ezekiel, it seems the promise got a little bigger. Now, it's up to me to try to find 'em and buy the freedom of his family."

Scratch let his gaze rest on the young man by the fire, looking as if he was peering into his soul and examining what kind of mettle from which this man was cast. As Jeremiah continued to stare into the fire, Scratch surmised that the young man's eyes held nothing but sincerity and heart-felt concern. There was no deceit, subterfuge, or anything that bore witness to any flaw in this man's character. Dropping his eyes to the dying flames, Scratch said in a soft voice, "My momma was a slave." A simple statement that forged a bond stronger than anything that came from the hottest fire of the biggest blacksmith was now cast between the two new friends. A common thread from the youth of both men, now made them more than friends, but brothers in search of something to repay a common debt made so long ago.

It was shortly after midnight when Scratch nudged Jeremiah to wakefulness with a mocassined foot to his side hidden under the buffalo robe. "O.K. Sonny, we got us full moon up thar that's showin' us the way. So, if'n ya wanna catch that there side wheeler, we better git us a move on!"

With a growl, a grunt, a scratch or two, a cough and a spit, Jeremiah finally rolled out of his covers. Neither man had shed his buckskins, so after taking care of morning chores, they were again dipping silent paddles in the waters of the Missouri river. Their quest would require several days of travel, tireless effort, and due diligence to overtake the steam powered side wheeler Yellowstone. The boat was built for and owned by the American Fur Company and seldom traveled this river this late in the season, but the higher than normal water levels enabled the company to make one last run for the early season furs gained in trade from the Blackfeet, Assiniboine and the few independent trappers. The plan of the duo was to travel long hours, often late into the night to gain on the boat. When the sidewheeler had to stop for the night because of the many sand bars and rapids in the lower water, the canoe could easily navigate the more perilous waters. They were certain they would be able to catch up to the boat no farther downstream than Council Bluffs. The bourgeois at Ft. Union had told them the boat would be meeting a pack train from the fall rendezvous at Pierre's Hole when they docked at Council Bluffs and would wait there until the pack train showed.

The silver orb of the moon seemed to skip across the treetops as it followed them downstream, providing just enough light to enable them to avoid the few boulders, piles of driftwood snags, and other obstacles to their journey. With the smaller craft keeping closer to the bank, the water was lower but the current just as swift as the middle of the stream. After about four hours of travel, the rising sun began painting the hillsides and giving clarity to the river travelers. When Scratch's stomach began to rumble louder than the rapids, he spoke to Jeremiah, "Hey, young 'un, let's keep an eye out for some breakfast. It'll probly be on four legs, so if'n you see sumpin', either shoot it or give me a sign and I'll do it. I'm so hongry, my belly button's a pinchin' my backbone!" It was the best time of day for animals to come to the river for their riverside graze and morning drink and the last place they would expect danger would be on the water.

As the canoe rounded a big bend in the river, Jeremiah spotted a trio of deer getting a drink at the edge of a sandbar. With a quiet sign to Scratch to bring the boat to the bank, Jeremiah reached back to his pack and pulled out his cherry wood bow and quiver of arrows. The deer had not spotted the men and Jeremiah quickly strung the bow, nocked an arrow, and from the kneeling position in the bow of the canoe, let fly the arrow. The shaft sunk itself in the neck of the nearest and largest of the three doe causing it to jump back and seek to escape. Three steps brought it to its knees and then down. The other two deer quickly fled to safety. "Whoooeee, I guess you livin' with them 'rapaho musta done some good. That was sure 'nuff some good shootin'!" said Scratch, as he paddled the canoe to the current and down to the sandbar. "You shot it, I'll skin 'er out and cut us some strips, while you get a fire goin' I think I could just 'bout eat this whole thing, hair 'n all," observed the cheerful Scratch.

After eating their fill, and not wanting to take any additional time to smoke the remainder, the two wrapped the larger portions of meat in some cloth scraps and returned to their journey. Jeremiah observed the way Scratch was able to devour so much at one sitting, he assumed that the meat wouldn't last very long anyway. The two men had developed a pattern of movement that was completely in sync that made the canoe slip across the water smoothly and quickly. For three days, their travel was without incident and the evening of the third day, Council Bluffs came into view. As they continued their deep paddle strokes, they observed the Yellowstone tied off to two large cottonwoods on the bank with the gangplank stretched to the sandbar and there appeared to be little activity near the boat. The men agreed to put in a little upstream and go the rest of the way on foot to make their arrival as inconspicuous as possible.

Chapter Seventeen: Steamboat

THE FEW WISPY CLOUDS seemed to gather in the West to pay homage to the dying sun. Aiding the creator as He painted the sunset, the clouds captured and held the colors and extended themselves from plains to distant mountains to reflect off the early season dusting of white. With the world tinted shades of orange, the travelers made camp in a dense grove of sycamore, willows, and cottonwoods that extended from the water's edge to the upper bluffs. A quick gathering of driftwood and broken branches provided Jeremiah the fuel for the evening preparation of a meal. Scratch unloaded the canoe and placed packs and gear and bedrolls for the night's stay.

As the two set about devouring the strips of venison, pan bread, and coffee, Jeremiah inquired, "I thought this was s'posed to be a town, or village or sumpin'. All there be is that shack or lean-to or whatever it's s'posed to be, and those Indian huts or whatever they are. Where's the town?"

"Wal, the way I unnerstan' it is, this here meetin' of the Platte and Missouri was called Council Bluffs cuz of them bluffs here round 'bout, and they say that them explorers, Lewis and Clark, had some kinda council here wit' the Injuns some years back," responded Scratch.

"Ya think the Indians that are in those two camps up on the bluffs are friendly?"

"Course they is. If they weren't, they'd probly done killed ever'body 'n burnt the boat and ever'thin'" observed Scratch.

With a shrug of his shoulders, Jeremiah rolled into his bedroll in anticipation of a good night's sleep. Both men would sleep light and have weapons close at hand, but they anticipated no trouble and looked forward to a longer night of rest than they had enjoyed so far on the trip. Scratch had the coffee going, meat frying, and set about waking Jeremiah with the loudest belch he could muster. Startled at the unexpected sound, Jeremiah sat up faster than a whistle pig could hide with pistol in hand looking for the source of the attack. "Wha . . .where . . .??"

Sitting on the log across the fire from Jeremiah, Scratch emitted a cackle and a giggle that caused him to grab his ribs and roll backwards off his seat. Picking himself up and trying to regain whatever composure he had, he laughed and pointed at Jeremiah and said, "Boy, if'n you don't beat all. I sware you sure can move when yore scairt!"

"I wasn't scared. Just surprised, that's all."

"You was so scairt, yore eyes looked like fried eggs, they was so big an' white!" With another chuckle, he handed a tin of venison and bread with a cup of coffee to Jeremiah. "Come on 'n eat them vittles so we kin git on over to that trader 'n see just what's goin on."

The front of the shack was a cobbled mess of driftwood and cottonwood logs held together with strips of rawhide, rope and anything else the scrounger could find. The back half was a dingy lean-to type of canvas usually used by miners or other early travelers. Jeremiah wondered to himself if it was safe to walk into the feeble structure. As they entered, their nostrils were assaulted with an unidentifiable blend of odors that made for an almost suffocating stench. One small table sat against the longest wall with two stumps for chairs, two barrels held a large plank with mysterious origin and made up the bar or trading counter, whichever purpose was needed. What looked like a third barrel growled from behind the bar and said, "What'll it be, gents?" Jeremiah noted the talking barrel was just as soiled as the two barrels holding the plank, and stunk even worse. The appearance and smell didn't seem to bother Scratch as he said, "Got 'ny whiskey?"

"None for me, Scratch. I'm goin' to see to our packs and stuff. I'll be right outside," said Jeremiah, turning to the door and stepping out. His partner watched him leave and turned to strike up a conversation with the barkeep. Reaching for the tin cup now half full of trade whiskey, he asked, "So, how long that there boat been here?" Knowing most barkeeps were loose tongued, Scratch began his conversation of inquiry.

As he left the den of stench, Scratch noticed Jeremiah standing at the edge of the bluff overlooking the tied off boat. He made his way to his friend's side and asked, "Have ya figgered out how ya gonna skin this hyar varmit?"

"Nope. I ain't too good at plannin' things out, so I just have to take it as it comes," replied his youthful partner. "It's worked pretty good so far."

"Well, I spose that's all right. Cuz, when ya ain't got a plan, ya have ta pay purty close 'tention or ya git your tail in a knot. Course, if'n ya knew whatcha was doin' afore hand, things might work out a little better. Take fer 'sample, them injuns over there. The only thing they know is they're gonna git drunk. They plan it, and they do it. But then there's them that just do it. They all end up drunk. But when yore wantin' to do sumpin' more important than gittin' drunk, ya might wanna chew on it a little, 'fore ya try ter swaller it. Know what I mean?" Turning to face his friend, Scratch put a hand on Jeremiah's shoulder and turned him back towards the trader's shack. "Now, lookee over thar. Them injuns over yonder, they's Otoe's. They're the ones with the funny hair that looks like they been half scalped and got so scairt the rest of the hair stood up straight. That bunch really like their likker, and those that didn't go on the big hunt, stayed here just ta git drunk. And they do. Now, look at that village over yonder. That bunch is just an advance scout fer the rest of their tribe. Ya don't see them gittin' drunk cuz they got a job ta do and they ain't got a taste fer likker like them other'ns. That bunch there's gonna do o.k. fer themselves, too."

"So, what's the difference? What tribe are these over here?" asked Jeremiah.

"Wal, them's Potawatomie. And they're movin' their whole shebang down thisa way."

Jeremiah's sudden turn, quick intake of air, and hard squint of his eyes startled Scratch. "Dang, boy, what'd I say that got yer dander up?"

"It was Potawatomie that killed my mother and burnt us out of our home," came the stern reply through the taut jaws of Jeremiah.

"Whoa now, son. Don't go startin' another fight. We cain't handle that many at one time," warned Scratch.

"Yeah, I know, it's just . . . come'on, let's get our stuff down to the boat and see if we can't get on board."

As they made their way down the trail off the bluff, Jeremiah admired the biggest boat he had ever seen. It was 120' stem to stern, had a huge paddle wheel on each side, two decks and storage below. The white painted water beast looked like it could conquer any body of water and go anywhere it wanted. The inexperienced eye of Jeremiah didn't see any fault, and admired the craft with anticipation of the waiting adventure. Stopping at the end of the gangplank, the two bearded men looked every part the mountain men they were. Hailing the bridge, they asked if they could get passage downriver and were pleased with the response as the captain leaned out of the doorway and hollered, "Of course, come'on aboard!"

Making his way down to greet the newcomers, the captain altered between stepping down the stairs and lifting his feet to slide with his weight on the handrails. It was evident that was a practiced maneuver as he landed on his feet with a smile on his face. Not a very tall man, what he lacked in height he made

136

up in width with an appearance that resembled a ball more than a man. Short legs supported the rotund figure that was topped by an ear to ear smile under a captain's cap while a dark blue double breasted peacoat pulled at brass buttons as it stretched across his girth. His jovial manner exuded itself as he again greeted the two boarders. "Welcome, welcome. I'm Captain Anson Bennett, so, how can we be of service to you gentlemen?" Without waiting for a response, he continued, "Are you part of the rendezvous rag-tag that we've been waitin' on? Where's all the gear?"

A wide-eyed Scratch looked the captain over as he waited for an opening to answer the questions. "Uh, nope. We ain't with no rag-tag bunch. We be travelin' all by our lonesome and we're lookin' to go downriver a spell. Got room for a couple more?"

As his brow furrowed he glanced from Scratch to Jeremiah and said, "Sure, sure. We have plenty of room. How far are ya' goin'? Is this all your gear or do ya' have more somewhere?" The disappointment at their not being who he was waiting for had dampened his enthusiasm a bit.

Scratch gave Jeremiah an exasperated look that said, "*You talk to him, if he ever shuts up.*"

Jeremiah stepped forward and replied to the captain, "Well, first, we need to go at least to St. Louie. And yes, this is all our gear, 'cepin' for a canoe. Would it be all right if we bring it along?"

"A canoe ya say? Sure, sure. So, did you fellas come down the Platte or the Missouri?

"This river right here, ain't that the Missouri?" stated Jeremiah as he motioned to the water with his chin, a habit he picked up from the Arapaho. "We came from up by Ft. Union and been travelin' a spell. We've been following somebody. Do you have anyone on board with a gimpy leg, wearin' a boot that's kinda built up a bit?"

Scratch scowled at Jeremiah not wanting to give away the purpose of their travel, without knowing where others stood on this issue he thought it careless to let their hunt be known. The captain looked the two over before answering in a lower voice and with what could only be described as a cross between a scowl and a look of fear on his face, "Are you friends of his?"

"Well captain, I'm takin' a bit of a chance tellin' you all this but the man we're huntin' killed my partner and robbed the two of us before takin' out with some other renegades and killin' several others on their way to Ft. Union. We almost caught up with him there, but he jumped this here boat and we took out after him."

The captain turned and leaned over the white rail before continuing. "Ya know, travelin' on the Mississippi, I've seen some bottom feedin', trash eatin' catfish that were ugly enough to scare the daylights outta ya, and they were mean enough and had a big enough mouth to swallow just about anything whole with nary a thank you to be said." Scratch and Jeremiah looked at each other and back at the captain as they leaned back against the same rail. The captain continued, "Ya know, I'd rather take one of those ugly catfish into my bed before I'd want to travel another mile with that low-life piece of pond scum! You know what that piece of garbage did? He wasn't on board two days before he got into an argument with one of the hands, accused him of stealing, and cut him up and slit his throat before you could say Mississippi. Nobody saw it or heard it and it was just his word, so we couldn't really do anything about it, but just his bein' here has put my entire crew on edge. And on top of all that, he's been playin' poker with some of the other passengers, and they're scared to death of him too! He ain't that big, he's just so dang ugly and mean that nobody wants ta git near him!"

"Yup, that sounds like the one we're after. From the trail we been follerin' with dead bodies an' all, it's right that you and your crew do your best to avoid him. We just need a couple things from you captain. First, don't tell him we're here, he wouldn't recognize us anyway, and tell us where he's bunkin'," asked Jeremiah.

"Sure, glad to oblige. If you take care of that problem for me, you can ride all the way to St. Louis and I won't charge you a thing. He's in cabin 6 with two others, I think they'd like to git rid of him too." As the captain started to turn away, his gaze rested on some men standing at the edge of the bluff and waving to the boat. It was the pack train from the rendezvous that he had been waiting for and turning to Jeremiah he said, "Looks like they're here, so we'll get started loadin' and might even be headin' out in a bit. Go ahead and git your canoe aboard, put it on the stern behind the boiler, there's room there now, but this bunch will be stackin' their packs back there too." With that, the captain headed for the gangplank and up the bank to ramrod the loading of the boat.

To Keep a Promise

Chapter Eighteen: Confrontation

THE CAPTAIN HAD OFFERED a cabin to Jeremiah and Scratch, but they both agreed that stretching their bedrolls at the stern of the boat would be more to their liking. Neither man had slept under a roof of any kind for a long time. For Jeremiah, it had been back to the time of Ezekiel sharing the cabin, and for Scratch much longer. The idea of being confined to a small space with two or more other men and no fresh air and stars was closer to a prison than comfort.

The American Fur Company traders and workers wasted no time in getting the many packs, panniers, and furs aboard with most of it stacked on the stern portion of the boat. Although there was some stowage below the main deck, the captain didn't want to overload due to the low waters and the six foot draft of the boat. Jeremiah helped the workers and crew and made it a point to arrange the bales of fur so he and Scratch could use them for their bedrolls. Scratch pulled alongside in the canoe and hailed his partner, "Hey youngun', grab hold hyar and steady it up so I can git aboard." Jeremiah squatted down and reached for the prow of the craft to steady it so Scratch could roll his carcass aboard. The two then easily lifted the lightweight birchbark up and secured it atop the stack of panniers from the rendezvous. Most of the packers, traders and workers from the pack train made themselves busy stowing their personal gear in their cabins or on the deck space chosen for their journey. Others had already made their way to the forward cabin area for their first experience at a shipboard prepared meal. While most were thinking of food, the captain and crew got the ship underway on the muddy Missouri.

The captain had utilized the foremost cabin near the prow of the boat as the kitchen. The simple meals were prepared by the crew for passengers and crew and often amounted to no more than beans and cornbread and occasionally whatever meat was available. When the meal was ready, each man picked up their tin plates and cups, went through the line and crewmembers piled their plates with available food and poured the coffee. The two crewmembers that drew galley duty on this day were two black men, one with considerable scars showing on his bare arms and the other with scraggly chin whiskers. Some of the diners returned to their cabins while others made their way to the prow or stern to be seated on bales or boxes and some stood at the rail to partake of their repast.

In the meal line, two men separated Scratch and Jeremiah from Frenchy DuBois. Scratch gave Jeremiah a stern look and with a mumbled whisper, said, "Easy boy, easy now. We need to take our time and pick our spot." Jeremiah's rumbled grunt was the only acknowledgement given as the two men filled their plates and turned to the stern of the boat. Taking seats on a bale of furs, setting their plates on a large wooden crate, the men turned to each other and started to talk. Looking over Jeremiah's shoulder, Scratch saw Frenchy making his way to join them, and greeted him jovially. "Join us friend. We gots lots of room, hyar 'bouts. I'm Scratch and this youngun' here is Jeremiah, what's yore handle?"

"I'm Lucuque DuBois, course most just call me Frenchy. You fellas trappers?" inquired the renegade leader.

With a mouth full of beans, Scratch looked up at the Frenchman and nodded his head and mumbled "Ummhumm."

"Where 'bouts you do your trappin'?"

"Um, mostly the upper reaches of the Missouri, in Blackfeet country. We were up there on the Milk and the Beaver, spent last winter with them Blackfeet at them thar Sleepin' Buffler Hot Springs. One winter's 'nuff fer any man. Gets too cold up thar ta spend 'nother winter, so we be headin' fer warmer climes."

Scratch knew Frenchy was checking to see if these were the ones that had dogged his trail from the Absarokas. Since Scratch had done just what he told Frenchy, even though Jeremiah hadn't been with him, it was a believable story.

"You fellas got a cabin, or are ya sleepin' outside?" quizzed the Frenchman.

"Nah, we like the stars too much ta put a roof over our head. We just bed down out hyar," added Scratch, now not sure what Frenchy was getting at but playing along anyway.

The Frenchman pushed the beans around on his tin and commented, "This food ain't much, and havin' those damn darkies dishin' it up sure doesn't do my appetite very well."

"How so?" asked Scratch.

"They can't be trusted. They'd put anything in the food, they don't care. All of 'em are shiftless bums and not worth the powder to blow 'em to kingdom come!" angrily spat Frenchy. Jeremiah looked to Scratch to watch his reaction, but Scratch acted like he heard this all the time and did not rise to the bait.

"Well, I dunno 'bout that. I ain't been around 'em much to know those things," replied the little mountain man and he sopped up the remains on his tin plate with the last piece of cornbread. Jeremiah and Frenchy were finishing theirs as well, and all three picked up their coffee cups at the same time and buried their faces in the round tin mask of a cup.

"Well, we might get us a little game of poker going after a bit, if you're interested. Probably get together up in the prow and use some of those crates," stated Frenchy as he eyed

Scratch to judge his response, then rose to return to his cabin in the forward part of the boat. Jeremiah and Scratch acknowledged his remark with a non-committal wave and turned away. Scratch said to Jeremiah, "Whooeeee, even if I didn't know what that feller was and what he done, I still wouldn't like him. There ain't nuttin' 'bout him that would even be appealin' to a ground rootin' badger. And they scavenge just 'bout anythin' but I'm certain sure they'd turn up their nose at that skunk!" Jeremiah slowly nodded his head in agreement.

"I'm gonna take a look 'round this boat. I just want to see what this things all about," mumbled Jeremiah as he stood and stretched. He moved to the walkway that surrounded the lower deck. As he stepped to the railing, he casually strolled between the cabins and the sidewheel that grudgingly turned and stirred the muddy waters below. A few steps further and he came to the stairway to the top deck which he mounted and made his way to the walkway past the bridge to the forefront of the top deck. He placed his hands on the rail and leaned against it as he surveyed the panorama of the Missouri river. He watched the white water capped waves retreating from the advancing prow and the ripples chasing one another along the sides of the hull only to be churned under by the massive sidewheels. The banks of the river modulated the landscape with abrupt rising bluffs, copses of sycamore and cottonwood trees, grassy banks that slid silently away to the empty plains. As his eyes catalogued and memorized the scenery, the rhythmic sounds of the water punctuated by the occasional call of a random meadowlark or turtle dove stirred the memories and dreams of his mind. Images of Broken Shield and Laughing Waters paraded before him with recollections of their many times together hunting, laughing, and sharing dreams and grand ideas. But the overwhelming image of Buffalo Thunder or Ezekiel crowded out the times of laughter replacing them with images of Jeremiah giving the covenant of freedom for his family. *I just wish I knew how I was going to get it done.* Without warning, the sidewheels slowed and the boat turned slightly toward the shore. They had passed a slight bend in the river and came upon a grass covered shoulder that enabled the boat to draw closer to the shore. With several large sycamores scattered and near the bank, the boat would have ample tie offs and deep enough water to anchor for the night.

Typically, when the steamboats stopped for the night due to an inability to maneuver the many obstacles and sandbars, the crew would restock the wood for the boiler fire. As dusk was threatening, the captain chose three of his crew to drop the gangplank and secure the needed wood. Jeremiah watched with interest as the skilled deckhands threw the ropes while others waded to shore to secure them to the larger trees. The chosen three were the two former slaves Jeremiah has seen in the chow line, and a burly white man stripped to his waist and revealing a hairy chest that would make a bear jealous. Jeremiah had casually strolled to the shore side of the boat and enjoyed the evening breeze and the colors of the setting sun. Not used to being idle, he paced from the prow to the stern and back again, all the while taking in the scenery so different from his distant mountains. The many deciduous trees that differed from the conifers of the high country, everything still so green and open, the difference causing something within to yearn for his snow capped peaks, the clear mountain air and the sky scratching pines.

A movement below caused his eyes to drop to the gangplank to see a shadowy figure going to the shore. His brow furrowed as he made his way to the stairway, he was thinking, *That was that slave hunter, Frenchy. Now what is he up to?* Jeremiah went to the stern to find Scratch and tell him where he was going. Scratch said, "Well, ya better take yore smokepole, cuz ya don't know what that skunk might be up to!"

"No . . . but I think I will stick my pistol in my belt, just in case. It's gittin' too dark ta see anything far enough away ta need my rifle," responded Jeremiah. With a nod to his friend, Jeremiah quickly went to the gangplank and followed Frenchy. His many treks in the woods with his Arapaho friends served

145

Jeremiah well as he stealthily followed Frenchy. The wood gatherers had gone to the bend in the river where the higher spring waters had deposited piles of driftwood and snags. As the big white man was making his way back to the boat pulling a large log and carrying another, the renegade slipped behind one of the larger sycamores while he passed. Jeremiah was no more than a stone's throw behind Frenchy as he crouched behind some willows to watch the Frenchman. A few moments later, the larger of the two blacks, the one with the whiskers, passed by dragging three sizable logs down the same path as did the white man. Jeremiah was still puzzled at the actions of the renegade.

As the last former slave came into view, it was easy to see he was struggling with a large armload of driftwood. Frenchy waited for him to pass, then quickly stepped behind him and with a move so fast it startled Jeremiah, Frenchy grabbed the black man over his mouth and drew a knife across his throat. The assailant let his victim drop to the sand as his load of wood clattered to the ground. With a grin that showed yellow teeth beneath the scraggly whiskers, the vile figure of a human knelt beside the wide eyed and bleeding man. Not willing to wait for him to bleed out, Frenchy raised his knife to deal the final blow when he heard a growl from behind him, "Drop it!" The predator whirled on his heels and turned to see Jeremiah standing with a pistol aimed at his head, while he calmly stood with a scowl on his face and disgust in his eyes.

"Whoa now. You don't want to shoot me over this piece of trash. He's worth a hundred dollars to me. Just wait till I get his ears off and I'll split the money with you. It'll be the easiest fifty dollars you ever made," pleaded Frenchy with his black eyes probing out from beneath his thick black brows.

"I said drop it!" Jeremiah refused to listen to any pleas for mercy or time and carefully watched the calculating scum before him. Like so many others that walked on the wrong side of the law and decency, Frenchy felt himself above those that did right and smarter than anyone else and he also thought that no one could get the best of him while he had a knife in his hand. Looking at Jeremiah, he tried to appear casual as he rose to his feet, feigned to turn away, then whirled to lunge at the younger man. Jeremiah expected just such a move and did not hesitate to pull the trigger on his flintlock pistol, the hammer dropped, the flint scraped the frizzen, sparks flew and nothing but a metallic click. Jeremiah dropped his eyes to his pistol in disbelief at the misfire and that instant imperiled his life. The knife wielding Frenchman swiped his knife from Jeremiah's right side to the left and laid open the loose fitting cotton shirt and drew blood across Jeremiah's midriff. The young man's quick intake of his stomach and pull back to rise on his toes saved him from having his guts spill to the sand. His reaction was to use the pistol as a club and brought it down on the side of the Frenchman's head, causing him to stagger back a step. With another lunge and a swipe from Jeremiah's left to right, the knife fighter sought to finish his gutting of his opponent.

With a move typical of his youth and practiced ability at close fighting with the Arapaho, Jeremiah grabbed the wrist behind the knife, dropped his useless pistol and brought his right hand to the same wrist. Quickly lifting the arm and wrist over his assailant's head, he brought it straight down with all his strength and snapped the arm of the would-be killer. He screamed like a piglet caught in the talons of an eagle, and said, "You broke my arm!"

"Yup. Now, watch this," Jeremiah said, as he plucked the knife from his hand, and dropping his arm to his knee then bringing it back up, he buried the knife past the hilt just beneath the ribs of the ugly little man. With an exhale of foul smelling breath and a spittle of blood, the Frenchman died, and Jeremiah let him drop to the sand next to his last victim.

To Keep a Promise

Chapter Nineteen: Changing

THE CAPTAIN STOOD beside the forward stowage door as he turned to Jeremiah and said, "Look, I'm grateful to you for purging our ship of that foul smelling scum and I know you told me he had stolen from you and your partner, but I can't just let you have all his stuff. It just wouldn't be right, ya know? What proof do you have that any of his stuff is your'n?"

"Cap'n, I don't want all his stuff, I just want what's mine. Now, what he got from us was two parfleches and one pair of saddlebags. You can tell it's mine cuz branded on the inside flap is PR 3:5-6. My partner, Ezekiel, said that was some Bible verse that said somethin' 'bout God showin' us where we should be goin'," stated Jeremiah with frustration evident in his tone. The captain gave Jeremiah a glance from the corner of his eye and said, "I know that verse, I believe its from Proverbs and says, 'Trust in the Lord with all thine heart; and lean not unto thine own understanding. In all thy ways acknowledge him, and he shall direct thy paths.' Yeah, that would be God showing you where to be goin."

Frenchy had asked the captain to store his packs and gear in the forward stowage for security purposes. He told him he had some valuable trade goods and didn't want any of it to go missing. The attitude he displayed toward the captain was just one of the many irritants the captain felt against the renegade. The captain looked from Jeremiah to Scratch and back again to Jeremiah, then turned to open the stowage door. There wasn't room for anyone but the captain as he searched the shelves and floor for the described articles. He grabbed two bags from the corner and slid them to the doorway, "Dagnabit, that one's kinda heavy, whatcha got in there anyways? Here now, let me look to see if that has that mark on it like you said," commented the captain as he slid the parfleche into the light. As he lifted the flap, he noted the brand exactly as Jeremiah described. He tried to get a look at the contents, but Jeremiah had knelt by the bag and flipped the flap back over the opening. Captain Bennett then turned to the second bag as Jeremiah said, "That one doesn't look familiar, I don't think that one's ours."

As the captain started to open the second bag, he commented, "Dang, this'ns a little ripe!" He undid the buckle on the leather strap and lifted the cover, withdrawing a bit due to the smell. "What the dickens?" he exclaimed. Then reached into the bag to withdraw a piece of twine to see what was attached. As the bag revealed its secret to the light, the captain recognized a stringer of black human ears threaded like beads on a necklace. Bennett dropped the grisly trophies back into the bag and quickly made his way to the rail as his stomach threatened to turn itself inside out.

Jeremiah said, "Ya know, I didn't rightly know what he meant when he said they were worth a hunert dollars and he'd share it. But now I see, apparently he could get some kinda bounty with those ears as proof. That's why he killed Ezekiel, and those two river guides from that Ft. VanBuren, and the two crew here on the boat. I figger there's more than that in that bag though, probably at least a couple dozen." The captain had returned to the side of Jeremiah, "Whooeee, if'n he'da stayed on, he'd probly tried to kill all my negroes. There's only four more, but I need 'em every one." The three men fell silent as each considered the evil of the man and the high price he had exacted by his mere presence.

"Wal, go 'head on and get the other two, they're in the corner there. Didn't know they'd be so dad blamed heavy! What'd you say was in them?"

"He didn't," retorted Scratch, "but he tol me it's just some stuff from their cabin and such. He's takin' it back to Ezekiel's famly."

The captain's curiosity had been sated after his grisly discovery and he didn't press the two more. He straightened up, secured the stowage door, and turned to the stairway to the bridge. Without any further discussion, he disappeared up the stairs. As Jeremiah lifted one parfleche and saddlebags, he motioned to Scratch to take the second parfleche as they both headed to their corner of the stern amid the bales of fur and panniers. They stowed the packages beneath a stack of panniers and covered the stack with their overturned canoe, then rolled out their bedrolls on the furbales to make everything look the way it was before they returned.

"Wal, Jeremiah, looks like ya done got a purty big part of your doin's took care of, what with gettin' yore stuff back. Whatcha gonna do now?" asked Scratch.

"Gettin' that stuff back is just a part of it. I had to get that so I could get the main thing done. My promise was to find Ezekiel's family and get them free. All I know is that Ezekiel said something about a Clay plantation somewhere near Lexington, Kentucky."

"That shore seems like a mighty tall order. Course, if ya had somebody hepin ya that knew the area, it might be a little easier," observed Scratch.

"Didn't you say you were from there?" asked Jeremiah.

"Did I say that? Wal, ya know, come ta think on it. I believe yore right. Now yore a pretty smart young'un," kidded the older mountain man with a gap-toothed grin obscuring most of his face. "But, have ya figgered out how ya gonna be doin' it? Ya cain't just walk up to 'em and say, Hey, gimme them thar negroes. People git shot fer less'n that," stated the self-appointed philosopher. Scratch was gauging the commitment of Jeremiah after the milestone of gaining the return of his property. He didn't know exactly what the bags held, but he was certain the value was considerable and would be the source of the purchase price of the slaves. Scratch had put serious thought to the task ahead and had begun to formulate a plan based on his own history of the area and the known practice of slave-traders and slave-holders. He knew it would not be easy but he believed with the right planning and knowledge, it would be possible to find and free the family of Ezekiel as Jeremiah had promised.

"Wal, the way I look at it, it seems ta me, ya need to kinda change the way ya look an act. Ya see, ya'l be doin' bizness with the gentry an' they'd just look down on some 'un like you. I'm thinkin' we need ta kinda clean ya up a bit. You know, some new clothes an all. Make ya look like somebody that needs them thar slaves. Sompin' else, I know this fella thereabouts that kin' help us out cuz he knows most folks 'roun thar and he kinda knows what we ought ta be doin' to git them folks freed up, ya see," mused Scratch, as he matched his name and scratched his chin whiskers before he stuck a corncob pipe between his teeth.

Jeremiah watched with wide-eyed wonder as Scratch filled his pipe with tobacco and lit it and exhaled a cloud of smoke. The only time Jeremiah had seen a pipe was when the Arapaho elders had sat in council and passed the carved soap stone pipe around the circle with much ceremony. Scratch noticed the young man's wonderment and smiled through another white cloud, "Whattamatta boy, ain't ya never seen nobody smokin' afore?"

"Well, yeah, when the Indians had a council and passed the pipe. But I ain't never seen a white man do it, and a little'n at that."

"Ya wanna try it?" offered Scratch.

"No. That thing stinks! And if I wanted to suck on some smoke, I'd do it over a campfire, at least a campfire don't smell like that. Say, what'd you mean make me look like somebody that needs a slave, you know, with new clothes and all that?"

"Wal, ya know, like a gen'leman with money. Cuz, ya cain't just go take the slaves, folks call that stealin' and you'd git yore sef in a heap a trouble. So, ya gotta buy 'em and to buy 'em ya gotta talk to them what's got the money and talk 'em inta sellin'. Tell ya what, you just think on it, and while yore thinkin' ya just kinda watch for them thar fellas that strut 'round like fancy peacocks and how they act an such. When we gits ta town, we'll git ya outfitted and then we'll see what we need ta do next," mused Scratch. "In the meantime, I think we need ta be sure to watch o'er this stuff and one of us needs ta stay hyar all the time. Dontchathink?"

"Yeah, I do. There's no tellin' what that curious captain might say about these bags and there's too many on board that wouldn't think twice about cuttin' somebody's throat for even a little bit of 'goin' ta town' money," replied Jeremiah. The tall trees on shore had obscured the remains of the sunset and both men readied their beds for the anticipated night's rest. It would be a challenge for the mountain men to gain sleep as they were not used to the movement of the boat, even though the anchorage and tie-offs to the shore stabilized it, the current of the river still moved the craft with a lazy rhythm. But the lapping of the waves and steady rocking of the boat soon erased the wakefulness of the pair of buckskin clad adventurers.

"Jeremiah, da most impo'tant thing in my life, is da freedom of my fambly. That's the whole reason I do ever thin' I do. Cuz I wants my momma ta know what freedom is. She ain't neva' been able ta do what she wants, when she wants ta do it. Allus' been sumbody else tellin' her whats ta do. That ain't right! Ya gotta hep me git 'em free. Don't forget ya done promised!" The mountain of a black man stood before him wrapped in a buffalo robe with his braided hair falling to his broad shoulders, the fringed buckskins topping his beaded moccasins and his flintlock rifle cradled in his arms across his chest. The deep rolling of his voice that seemed to echo from the mountains, recalled the name he was known by among his adopted Arapaho, Buffalo Thunder. The startled Jeremiah jerked himself awake and he almost rolled off the bale of furs. The sudden movement drew a whisper from his partner, "Hold on thar boy, don't let it buck you off." With a grunt, Jeremiah flopped over on his side and pursued the elusive sleep, but the image of Ezekiel would not easily retreat from his consciousness. As his mind traveled the corridor of his memories of the day's events, the jumble of thoughts and the continual rocking of the giant cradle finally lured him to sleep. Unknown to Jeremiah, but watched by Scratch, a bearded man slipped back around the boiler and disappeared to the front of the boat.

Chapter Twenty: Outfitting

AS THE *YELLOWSTONE* APPROACHED St. Louis, many of the passengers crowded the rails to take in the sight of the westernmost seat of civilization, Jeremiah and Scratch among them. It had been more than a decade since Jeremiah and his dad had outfitted here enroute to the mountains and the changes were many. When they visited before there were no steamboats, and now there were seven already tied off to the levee that their sidewheeler was approaching. Sometimes two abreast, the towering smokestacks, large stern wheels, and long gangplanks of the many boats made a virtual forest of confusion and amazement. Most showed little activity, but several were akin to a beehive with crew members and stevedores of every shade of color loading or unloading cargo and passengers. Set back from the levee, an odd assortment of buildings from single level to three stories with a variety of windows, most too dirty to see through, and each bearing a sign or signs either painted across the false fronts or dangling in the wind that screamed out the manner of business housed there and bore testimony to the variety of trades practiced. A few of the buildings had a fresh coat of paint, but most had a mixture of colors peeling off but adding to the character of the waterfront.

Earlier in the day, the two travelers consulted with Captain Bennett concerning their plan to go to Kentucky and their need to go ashore at St. Louis to take care of matters. The Captain had shared with them that the *Yellowstone* was going to make a few runs downriver for the remainder of the winter and they could go as far as the Ohio River with him, and they were only staying in St. Louis long enough to unload the rendezvous cargo and then head out to Cape Girardeau. The two men agreed to continue on the *Yellowstone* which made it easier to leave their trappings aboard and conduct their business in St. Louis. Now as the crew was tying off the boat at the levee, the travelers prepared to disembark.

With the saddlebags over his right shoulder, a parfleche on his left arm and his flintlock in his right hand, Jeremiah led the way to the gangplank followed by Scratch carrying the remaining parfleche and also bearing his smokepole. With his red and black Hudson bay capote, Scratch provided considerable contrast to Jeremiah and his buffalo hide long coat that still bore fur on the shoulders, but both of the men and their attire were obviously from the mountains to any passersby. Scratch observed, "Too many dang people fer my likin', and there ain't nary a breath of fresh air in this whole dadgum place. Whoooeee, the stink 'round chere, lookee thar, they just dump their leavin's right in the road fer anybody to step in. Why the only varmints what does that in the mountains is them that wears some fur!"

Nodding his head in agreement and emitting a bit of a chuckle, Jeremiah said, "You're right 'bout that. Let's just git our bizness done and git on down the river. We got a lot ta git done and a long ways to go before we can get back to our mountains, and it won't be soon enough for me." They followed a walkway in front of the commercial buildings to a corner of the street marked with a small black and white sign that read "Olive St." As they turned to follow the walkway towards the business part of town, Scratch glanced over his shoulder at a man that appeared to be following them but as Scratch turned his head, the man ducked into a doorway. Dismissing it as nothing, he continued to follow Jeremiah up the slight incline of the street and walkway. With the rapid growth of the city, the water and sewage system was being installed and several of the downtown streets had been paved with cobblestones. Others were still undergoing the construction leaving most a muddy mess and even foot traffic was limited, but near the waterfront there was no shortage of people going every which way on the narrow streets and walkways. Two men, obviously drunk, stumbled out of a pub in front of the mountain men. Noticing the travelers, one of the drunks called out, "Hey thar, whatcha got in them bags boys? Ya wanna share?" In answer, Scratch yelled back, "I got my dirty underwear. Ya wanna wash it fer me?" Both men looked at each other and turned away without any more comment.

The two men still had four or five city blocks to go to their destination, the First Commercial Bank of St. Louis. As they passed the entry to an alleyway, Scratch's sideways glance caught sight of another shadowy figure that appeared to be following. He whispered to Jeremiah, "Hey, I think we gots some comp'ny, keep yore eyes peeled." Jeremiah casually lifted his rifle to rest the barrel across his left arm and brought the hammer to full cock and continued walking. Scratch had already readied his rifle for action and matched Jeremiah step for step. "Them two drunks are behind us, so I'm thinkin' we'll see somebody up front real soon. I'll take these two so yore job's in front of ya," cautioned Scratch.

A short stone's throw brought them to a narrow space between buildings that belched forth the man that had been following them. Jeremiah recognized him as one of the packers from the crew with the rendezvous. With a wave of his pistol, the thug demanded, "Gimme them bags!" With his rifle pointed to the street and the bandit hugging the building,

Jeremiah knew he wouldn't be able to bring his rifle to bear. He lowered the parfleche and asked, "These bags?" and with a slight backward swing, he brought it forward and threw it at the robber. The weight of the bag was unexpected by the thief and he was knocked to his back giving Jeremiah the opening to jump astraddle of the assailant and bring the barrel of his rifle across the man's throat. At the same time, Scratch spun to his left and fired a 50 caliber lead ball into the chest of the larger of the two drunks. The third man quickly realized the easy marks had overcome the odds which caused him to drop his pistol and turn and run down the street. Jeremiah said through gritted teeth, "I hate a thief." His attacker lay motionless and appeared dead, but the slow rise of his chest showed signs of life. Jeremiah rose to his feet, picked up his parfleche and said to Scratch, "Well, I guess we needed a little exercise." Leaving the two thugs where they fell, the two mountain men renewed their walk to the bank.

The manager was skeptical of the two buckskin clad and bearded men as they set the parcels on the floor beside his desk. His manner quickly changed when he realized the amount of gold dust contained in the bags, and he began to treat the two men with excess courtesy and respect. When their business was completed, Jeremiah clutched four leather pouches with gold coin, handed one to Scratch and said, "Hold on to that for us." Most of the gold had been deposited in the bank and Jeremiah was given a certificate of deposit from the manager who explained the process of issuing a bank draft for any future withdrawals. "We are here to serve you sir. So, anytime you need anything, you just let us know," he stated and he nodded and shook their hands.

As they exited the bank, Scratch said to Jeremiah, "I knew ya had some dust in them bags, but dang boy, that's a powerful lot a money. Even what we're carryin' is a bunch."

"Well, like you said Scratch, we need to be buyin' some things, and it'll take a pretty good sum to get Ezekiel's family free."

158

Jeremiah had tied two of the bags together with a long leather strap which he draped over his neck letting the bags hang to the sides of his chest under his shirt. The third bag was draped over his belt with the weight inside the top of his pants. Scratch likewise hung his one bag from his belt inside his pants top. The two made their way to 5th street following directions from the banker. As they neared their destination, they noted the sign that read, "Men's Haberdashery." Jeremiah said, "What is a haberdashery?" He watched two uniformed soldiers walk into the storefront, "What are you getting' me into, Scratch?"

"Oh, hold yer horses sonny boy, I tol' ya we needed tag it ya outfitted. This hyar place will do that fer ya," commented the grizzled mountain man as he stepped into the clothing store. They were greeted by a clerk attired in pants and matching waistcoat, with exposed and rolled up shirtsleeves and a measuring tape draped over one shoulder. He had a bald head with a half halo of grey hair just over his ears, a slight pot belly fighting against the tight waistcoat, and half-round spectacles perched on his round red nose. Looking over the lenses at the newcomers, the clerk cleared his throat and said, "Yeeesssss?"

After just over two hours, both men had been completely outfitted with the latest fashions in men's attire. Scratch had protested, but when Jeremiah said if he didn't Jeremiah wouldn't either and after all, the overseer had to look as good as the plantation owner, the roles that were deemed necessary for the accomplishment of the task before them. Choosing not to wear the new clothes, both men were again attired in their comfortable buckskins, complete with powder horns, possibles bags, and flintlock rifles. The previously emptied parfleches and saddlebags were now filled with the new clothes and accouterments enabling the men to settle up, carry their packs, and return to the boat.

They arrived on board just minutes before the captain started barking orders to get the boat underway. It was late afternoon but the captain wanted to put the city behind him and get a few miles downriver before putting in for the night. The boiler had already been fired up and a new stock of wood put aboard as the sidewheels began the familiar churning of the water to move the boat back into the current of the big muddy. A young black man had been stationed at the prow of the boat to watch for any floating obstacles in the way with instructions to promptly sound any warning. Another man was taking the soundings on the depth of the water as the boat moved away from the shore. Within the hour, the city's skyline had disappeared and the structures on the shoreline were fewer and farther between. As the dusk approached, the captain ordered the crew to make ready to go ashore and tie off the boat. The few hours of travel had distanced them from the crowds, sounds, and smells of the city and the travelers again drew deep breaths of the fresher air of the countryside.

Chapter Twenty-One: Rivers

THE TWO MEN rhythmically dipped their paddles in the muddy water of the Ohio river and easily pulled the canoe upstream. The last days travel onboard the *Yellowstone* passed quietly and the men had disembarked after the captain had put the boat in at the dock of Cape Girardeau. It was a short distance below the Cape to the confluence of the Ohio and Mississippi and the men had easily traversed the few miles just this morning. Having made good time, they were looking forward to making it to Owensborough before nightfall. Jeremiah had commented to Scratch about the yellow bluffs on the Northwest side of the river. It was an unusual formation of stone and clay, with little variation in the color and the few small streams that cut through the banks were also colored by the clay. The captain had told the two men about the coloring and how the town had been named Yellow Banks before being changed to Owensborough.

Pulling the canoe ashore just a little downstream from the nearest buildings of the town, the dwindling light of dusk helped the men decide to bed down in the trees before entering the town. The cool air of the evening prompted Jeremiah to the quick building of a fire while Scratch hauled the packs to the campsite. As he spread out the bedrolls, the appointed cook put a fresh pot of coffee on the stone beside the fire and readied the last of their venison strips in the small frying pan. The smoke and jumping sparks from the campfire soon blended with the smells and crackling fat of the meat. Scratch took a seat on a large stone while Jeremiah tended the meal. "Hallo the camp!" came a cry from the darkening shadows of the nearby trees. "Can I come aboard?"

Scratch brought his rifle across his lap with the muzzle pointed in the direction of the cry and said, "Come ahead on, if yore friendly. If ya ain't, say yore prayers cuz yore 'bout ta meet yore maker!" A low hanging branch of the cottonwood pushed aside as a tattered old man waddled his way into the camp. His attire readily revealed that he was what was commonly known as a river rat, a man that had made his living on the boats but had fallen on hard times and had no way of providing himself so was forced to scrounge for scraps and handouts. With no perceived threat, both men relaxed their grip on their rifles and set them down within easy reach against the larger stones back from the fire.

"Wal, ol' timer, whatcha doin' out here this time a night?" asked Scratch.

"He he he, I was just sleepin' back yonder a ways, an' yore cookin' woke me up. Think mebbe ya could spare an ol' man a bite or two?"

"We're not in the habit of just giving our food away, but I tell ya what. Maybe we could swap a little," said Jeremiah. The old man's interest perked up and with a gleam in his eye and his lips parting in a somewhat toothless smile, he quickly nodded his head up and down.

"Sure, anything, whatcha need? I kin probly git just 'bout anythin' fer ya.?

"Well, all we need's a little information. You know much about this town up yonder?" inquired Jeremiah.

"Shore. I know ever thin' ya needs ta know. Whatcha want?" replied the old man.

The campfire suppertime conversation covered everything from details about the town and surrounding countryside to the history of river travel and the founding of the town. It was an interesting tidbit of history that Lewis and Clark had wintered here prior to departing on their famous travels. The old man shared more than he knew about the people of the town and the neighboring Indian tribes. "Yessir, since them dumb politicians passed that thar Indian Removal act, it's taken 'em a long time to git 'er goin' but the Injuns are a movin' on West. Them Cherokee and Chickasaw ain't waitin' fer no army escort. They's headin' West on their own account and timetable. Most of 'em was movin' this past summer, but they's still some stragglers on the move. If yore headin' East, ya'll probly run into some of 'em if ya ain't careful. Course, most of 'ems friendly enough, but some of 'em ain't too happy 'bout havin' ta leave their homes an all," mused the old man. It had been some time since he had sat around a fire and talked with other men, it made him feel good. He was also enjoying imparting his little bit of knowledge to the travelers.

The river rat had agreed to rejoin the duo as morning made its debut. Shortly after some warmed over left overs and enough coffee to float a good sized canoe, the three made their way to the nearby town of Owensborough. Although there wasn't much to the town, the river rat, now known as Thaddeus, directed them to the Livery as they came in sight of the first of the buildings. As usual, the first building on the edge of town was the Livery, consisting of a fair sized barn and stable that also housed a blacksmith forge and assorted gear. A corral with several animals adjoined the barn from which the smithy and owner now exited with a pitch fork loaded with hay for the animals. He hollered a greeting, "Howdy gents! Yore up n 'bout early this morning.' What kin I do ye fer?" he inquired with a hopeful look anticipating a bit of profitable business to start his day.

"Wal, we done decided that we were plum tired of walkin' and thot we might mebbe trade ya outa a horse or two ta remedy that sit'chiashun. Got anything besides them thar broken down ole farm plugs, do ye?" responded Scratch as he ambled towards the corral and put a foot up on the lowest log of the pole fence. He was followed by Jeremiah and Thaddeus who assumed a similar stance by the fence. The smithy leaned his fork against the barn and strolled to the fence to start the bickering. Jeremiah stepped back to let Scratch handle the negotiations and within about a half hour, the men were proud owners of a high spirited dapple grey gelding, a well set-up black mare and a bright eyed bay gelding. Included in the deal were two saddles, a pack saddle, and the additional tack necessary to outfit the duo comfortably.

They took possession of their new animals and led them up the street a short distance to the mercantile. Thaddeus had forewarned them that the owner of the mercantile was as cranky as they come, but honest as the day was long. Although the mountain men had made an offer for Thaddeus to join them, he declined with a remark about getting too far from the boat traffic. Jeremiah pressed a coin into Thaddeus hand, "That's ta keep ya goin' fer a while." And with that, the three men parted company.

As they stepped into the mercantile, they stopped a moment to let their eyes adjust to the dim light and to survey the goods stacked floor to ceiling. From somewhere behind a pile of goods near a narrow counter came a scratchy voice, "Whatcha want!" The two leaned side to side in an attempt to sight the source of the welcome and finally spotted a portly figure with hair going directions where there were no directions and a pot belly that strained at the slightly soiled long clerk's apron that reached just below the knees of the strange figure of a man. A scowl peered out of squinted eyes that were almost obscured by bushy eyebrows that fought for forehead space with the scraggly gray locks that tumbled from his top knot. Too red lips pursed between a red bulb and a chin that mirrored the round nose.

Scratch turned to Jeremiah with a grin as he sought to keep from laughing and a look that said, "You talk!"   Jeremiah turned to the man and said, "We've got a list here of some supplies we need." He stepped to the counter and leaned around the stack of boxes to look towards the man on the stool. The clerk twisted his rear end to slide off the stool and approach Jeremiah. "Lemme see that," he grunted. With a moan and a mumble, be began to worm his way through the piles and aisles picking up various items from the list.

"Ain't got no apples 'n such. Got some canned peaches though. Will that do?"

"That'll be fine," replied Jeremiah as he worked his way around the store eyeing whatever might come in handy. He occasionally picked up an item or two and added it to the stack by the counter. Near the side window, Jeremiah noticed a wall rack with rifles and a counter with pistols and other hunting gear, and made his way to view the goods. He motioned to Scratch to join him as he looked at the weapons on the wall rack.   "Hey, Scratch, those two rifles there in the middle of that rack. Are those the Hawken rifles you were talkin' 'bout the other day?" Scratch leaned over the counter to get a closer look and replied, "Yup, I believe they is," then turning to the front of the store he hollered, "Hey, storekeep, are these here rifles them Hawken ones we heerd 'bout?   With that the storekeeper came back to deal with the strange men clad in buckskins and looking out of place in town. It was unusual for a store to have the Hawken rifle in stock as most were custom made for the individual, but these had come in trade from a widow woman whose husband had ordered the rifles from the Hawken shop in St. Louis.   After another hour of discussion and bickering, one flintlock rifle and one flintlock pistol had been traded on two .54 caliber Hawken rifles, one Colt Paterson revolver pistol, two Bowie knives with scabbards, and assorted caps, powder, lead bars, molds and other shooting necessities. Scratch had insisted on keeping his smokepole flintlock, "Just in case." Together with the filled list of supplies, the men left the store loaded down with goods and a bit lighter in gold coin. The storekeeper was happy with the trades and purchases and especially happy with the gold coin, which was a rarity where most people dealt on credit and trade goods.

It took a little while to get most everything loaded on the one pack horse with the panniers and strapped to the pack saddle. The men had to keep the parfleche and saddle bags and bedrolls on their individual horses. Slipping their new rifles into the saddle scabbards, the men turned the horses to the road that led East from town. Both men stood tall in their stirrups and drew a deep breath of fresh country air. "Smell that? No mud, no fish, no city puke! Just good fresh air!" Jeremiah shouted to Scratch, as both men grinned as wide as a hungry possum.

Chapter Twenty-Two: Kentucky

THE WELL WORN TRAIL wormed its way through the thick forest whose floor was littered with layers of multi-hued leaves. The close growing hardwood trees stretched skeletal branches like fingers reaching for the low-hanging clouds overhead. Several of the tall gray wooden figures tenaciously gripped the remaining now brown leaves that decorated a few sheltered branches. Jeremiah's eyes roved continually from tree to tree and beyond, taking in the variety of trees never before seen by him. He was used to the coniferous forests of the mountains with thick pines and scattered mountainsides of aspen and stream fed ravines littered with towering cottonwoods. This abundance of differing hardwoods with bark and branches of rough texture and contoured trunks held Jeremiah spellbound. Along with the easy gait of the horses on the winding trail he felt the illusion of peace and quiet.

It had been a long day already but there was still more than an hour of daylight left when Scratch pulled the short convoy to a halt in a small clearing. Drawing up beside him, Jeremiah gave a silent but questioning look at Scratch as he started to dismount. Then vocalizing his ignored question, Jeremiah said, "So, whatcha doin' ol' man? I thought we was gonna keep on moving as long as we could see, so what's up?"

"Wal, I think we need ta git familiar with these new toys we got us back yonder. I don't fancy comin' on sumpin' where we need 'em and don't know how ta use 'em!"

Jeremiah slid off his mount and led his horse and the pack horse to the edge of the clearing as he responded to Scratch, "I was kinda thinkin' the same thing. But you know how us kids are with new toys, just cain't wait to play with 'em!"

The men quickly unsaddled and unpacked the horses, led them to a patch of grass and tethered them with enough lead rope to graze. Scratch walked as straight a line as possible through the trees and used his hatchet to mark a blaze on a tree that could be easily seen from the clearing. On his way back he stopped and cut another blaze closer to their campsite.

"That fer one's 'bout one hunert yards, couldn't git any further cuz of these dang trees bein' so thick. That close one's 'bout twenty five. So, load 'er up an see whatcha kin do."

Both men were natural marksmen and hit the mark with each shot. Their experience gave them the advantage in knowing range, drop, and accuracy of the .54 caliber balls with the measured powder behind them, but both were well surprised with the accuracy and consistency of the Hawken rifles. The Hawken had the reputation of better range and accuracy than the usual flintlock and with the percussion caps instead of the flint, they were more dependable. Pleased with their purchase, both men quickly gained confidence in their new weapons. Eyeing the blaze on the near tree and using an overhand throw Scratch hit the mark dead center with his new Bowie knife. "Ha! See if ya can top that young'un!" he challenged Jeremiah. Without a word but with a fluid motion underhand, Jeremiah buried the first two inches of his Bowie blade directly under Scratch's. Without any hesitation, Jeremiah pulled his new Colt Paterson revolver and fired twice at the same blaze with each ball hitting on opposite sides of the Bowie blade. "Waaagh! Wal, I'll be a one-eyed squirrel in a pine tree, that ain't haf bad!" commented the wily mountain man.

With play time over, the two men made short work of the evening meal and making ready for the night. This was just the first portion of the Kentucky part of their journey, but it was also the last part of the long trek from the mountains. Jeremiah expressed his curiosity as they sat near the dwindling campfire, "How much longer ya think it'll take us, Scratch?"

Taking a firebrand to light his pipe, he puffed a small cloud of white smoke, tossed the twig back into the fire and replied, "Wal, as near as I kin figger, couple a days'll put us in Bardstown, and from there to Lexington, mebbe another two or three days, dependin'" he surmised.

Jeremiah stared at the fire, tossed another twig in the flames, then looked up at Scratch, "I think I'm gittin' a little skeered, else there's a new batch a butterflies done took up residence in my gut. There's just so much ridin' on what we're 'bout ta do, ya know? It seems my whole life has been pointin' to this one big thing, keepin' that promise to Ezekiel. I can't let him down, I just can't." Scratch was at a loss for words and grunted and stood up to go to his bedroll. Jeremiah followed his example and also turned in for the night.

With just one shared pot of coffee and little conversation, the men began the routine of packing up their gear and readying the mounts for the days travel. Scratch noted Jeremiah's gaze as he surveyed the timber covered hillside then down to the valley below them. The view was somewhat restricted by the thick timber but with most trees bare of foliage, the terrain was reasonably visible. Scratch said, "We'll keep that ridge yonder to the North of us and follow this hyar trail. It's not as easy travelin' as the road down yonder, but there's shore a lot less bothersome folks. We'll be crossin a crik or two 'fore we gits to the Rough River and the timber'll thin out some and the goin' gits a lil' easier. Ol Thaddeus back yonder said we'd best keep an eye out fer some of them Cherokee or Chickasaw injuns. They's usually friendly, but what with the gov'n'ment a movin' 'em outta cheer they just might show us how mad they really is."

As the caravan of three horses and two men made their way on the trail, Scratch took advantage of the many opportunities to educate his companion on the names of different trees and plants in this territory that was so new to him. He called out the names of Tulip Poplar and Sassafras and told of the difference in the leaves, bark, and colors at different times of the year. "Now, down thar in the open areas ya'll see more of them Bur Oak with their long leaves that are yellow brown in the fall. Course, thars also some Oak and Peecahn, some Buckeye and Maple and some Birch. Now them Birch are kinda like them Quakies up in the Rockies, cepin' they gits a little bigger down cher."

For their noon stop they only fixed a pot of coffee and ate the last of the Pemmican remaining in their parfleches. They agreed on the need to replenish the meat supply whenever possible. Scratch told Jeremiah, "The deer 'round cheer are a bit different from them up in the mountains. These are Whitetail, they ain't got the big ears and they got a big ol' flag of a white tail and they is skittish as all git out. So, if'n ya see one, don't wait on him, take yore shot quik like." With that image before him, Jeremiah took the lead as the men continued on the trail. Scratch continued his woodlands education from the rear of the convoy as Jeremiah wondered how soon Scratch would tire of talking. *Maybe he's just excited about bein' back in his old stompin' grounds,* thought Jeremiah.

The remainder of the day yielded views of squirrels, raccoons, a couple of coyotes, and a quick glimpse of a couple of deer as they flagged and bounced their way through some thick brush too fast and too far for a shot for the pot. Scratch had fallen silent as dusk began to draw her gray skirts around them. As Jeremiah craned to get a better view of a clearing, he was startled by the crack of Scratch's Hawken as the shooter felled a good sized doe. But Jeremiah wasn't the only one startled, Scratch's bay gelding exploded under him. The bay switched ends in mid air coming down on his front feet with his head tucked in between them. Kicking his heels at the hovering cloud of gunsmoke, the gelding bent in the middle and threw his head back in an attempt to unseat his rider. When the horse twisted in mid air with his hind feet going North and his front pointing South, Scratch saw nothing but blue sky and grey clouds just before the ground rose up to rob him of his breath. When the dust settled, the bay gelding slowly walked over to Scratch and sniffed at him with an apologetic look coming from his big brown eyes. Scratch sucked in the dusty air and coughed and spit, then looked at the bay and said, "You dagnabbit good fer nuthin' flea bit cayuse, what'd ya do that fer?"

"I'd ask if you was O.K., but ya don't look none the worse fer wear. Ya gonna make it?" Jeremiah asked as he handed Scratch the Hawken that he dropped after the first jump. With a grumble that sounded like a momma bear, Scratch rolled to his side and rose to stand beside Jeremiah. "I just thot we should make camp rightcheer and that's th' only way I could git ya to stop. So, tether them horses and let's go git our supper," grunted the old timer. Jeremiah did as instructed and followed Scratch to the carcass of the felled deer. Leaning his rifle against a nearby tree, Scratch pulled his Bowie and knelt to start the butchering. Rolling the doe to its back and spreading the legs, his first cut with the razor sharp knife spilled the guts to the side and prompted Jeremiah to reach in the chest cavity and pull the remainder out. Laying the heart and liver to the side, he started to peel the hide back as he followed the stretched hide with the blade of the knife. His concentration was interrupted by Jeremiah as he whispered, "We got company."

Standing in the shadows at the edge of the clearing were three Chicksaw Indian braves, two holding nocked arrows with their bows and the third held a flintlock fusil rifle that was pointed to the ground. Attired in buckskin leggings and loose fitting bloused shirts, the men could have easily passed for dark skinned white men. The largest of the three had a three tiered bone necklace, long hair tied at the back and a possibles pouch strapped across his right shoulder. There was nothing to distinguish the other two but all three had somber expressions that betrayed their displeasure with the two white men. It was evident the three had been on the trail of the downed doe and without words but with sign language and facial expressions made their claim evident. Scratch motioned for them to join him and Jeremiah beside the deer and held out the liver to the apparent leader of the two. Without further word, Scratch pulled the skin back farther, cut out one of the backstraps and handed it to Jeremiah. Scratch then stood and motioned to the Indians to take the remainder of the carcass while he and Jeremiah turned to walk back to their hastily made camp. As the two men approached the clearing of their camp, their curiosity caused them to turn and see nothing but a gut pile where the three men and deer carcass had been.

As they stepped into the clearing, Scratch let out a big sigh of relief and said, "Boy, I've had about 'nuff excitement fer one day. Let's git some supper in our bellies, git some sleep, and git outta here!"

"I'm all for that," replied Jeremiah as he gathered some firewood. Scratch grabbed the coffee pot and started preparing the essential nectar of the mountain man. As the campfire flared to life, Jeremiah walked to the downhill side of the clearing and stared through the woods and watched the valley floor blossom with the campfires of the Chickasaw clan below. "Ya know, I think that's a darn shame what they're doin' to those Indians. Just cuz some dumb politicians want more land for themselves and their friends, they think they have to move the Indians out all because they write up a law and they think everybody else has to do what they say. There ain't nuthin' right about it. "

"Wal son, that's all the more reason for folks like us ta just do what we thinks right, no matter what them wig wearin' outlaws called politicians think! Ain't that one o' the reasons we're on this trip anyway? When one man makes a slave outta another, that ain't right neither. So, we just have to do what's right whether they like it or not!" expounded Scratch.

To Keep a Promise

Chapter Twenty-Three: Lexington

THE COOL AIR of the evening capped off another full days travel through the Kentucky countryside. It had been an uneventful day with little change in the terrain or scenery. The crossing of the Rough river was without incident and did nothing more than break the monotony of the days travel. Making good time and bypassing the settlement of Bardstown, the men made camp near the bank of Cox creek. It was a smooth running creek between grassy banks lined with towering Tulip Poplar trees and a scattering of Maple and Birch. The water was clear and deep and invited the men for a change of fare for their supper. Yielding to the suggestion, Scratch tossed in a line with baited hook while Jeremiah prepared the fire and coffee. For most of the trip, other travelers were scarce and seldom seen, but recently the appearance of others was not unusual. The two men made certain they were well off the trail and away from the roadway before making their solitude camp.

As Jeremiah finished rolling out the bedrolls and stepped back to the fire, Scratch came from the creek with a stringer of fish and a few greens to make the evening meal a pleasant change from the usual fare. After frying it all up in bacon grease, the men wasted no time in emptying the sizzling frying pan. After washing it all down with the usual coffee, both men leaned back against their respective logs and enjoyed the leisurely evening. It was Scratch's turn to lend to the melancholy and the glassy look of his eyes revealed the depth of thought swirling in his mind. Jeremiah asked, "So Scratch, what's got you so down in the mouth?"

"Aw, nuthin' I"se just 'memberin' my pappy. Did I ever tell ya 'bout him?" he inquired.

"Scratch, you ain't told me nuthin' bout yourself, 'cept that you were from this here country."

"Well, I know I tol' ya' my momma was a slave, but what I didn't say was that my father was her owner or master. He didn't want no kids and made her git rid o'me. So she took me inta town to a big ol' church there, it was a black church, and went to the pastor and talked him into takin' her kid or me that is. He did and he and his wife raised me up till I left in my late teens. I just wasn't cut out fer the city life and since I was half white and half black, I just didn't belong anywhere. So, when I went West, it was just easier to be a white man and I never looked back. Until now, that is."

"And that's where we're going when we get to Lexington?" asked Jeremiah.

"Yup. He knows most everybody and he'll know what we need to do to get Ezekiel's family and he'll also know what to do after."

"After? What do you mean after?" asked Jeremiah.

"Wal, ya didn't think that'd be the end of it, didja? Just cuz ya buy 'em, don't mean you can just set 'em adrift. If they stay 'roun here, some other plantation owner or farmer or factory owner would claim they had escaped and put 'em right back ta work."

"Humm, I hadn't thought about that, but I guess you're right. So ya think your pappy will know what we'll need to do?" asked Jeremiah.

"Yeah, there's ways ta take care of that and he'll know who and how to git it done. Don't worry, we can count on him," responded Scratch. "I think if we git a early start, we can probably make Lexington tomorrow evening. Then we can git us a room and git all citified before we go see my pappy the next morning.'"

The Second Street Inn, an unpretentious two story brick building with an entrance of nothing more than a single step and broad white door and a simple sign, fit the bill for what the two men were looking for to spend the night in and start the new chapter of this event. Just a block off the main street and near the primary business area, it was also within close walking distance from the livery stable. It was the liveryman that recommended the inn and bragged on the table fare and the company. "Just you stay away from that sweet little brown haired girl, Suzie, cuz she be my girl, ya hear?" stated the broad shouldered blacksmith named Sam, with a broad smile that revealed a mouth full of crooked and browned teeth.

When they secured their room, Jeremiah leaned to the door to look into the dining room and get a glimpse of little Suzie, then chuckled to himself thinking, *Now those two certainly make a pair. If they ever have kids. . .* as he pictured the progeny of the two rather large possible parents. As they climbed the stairs, Scratch said, "Wal, believe it or not, I'm kinda lookin' for'd to that bath and shave. It's been a while .. ." to which Jeremiah replied, "Yes, it certainly has. But I think it will do us both good. We probably won't even recognize each other without these many layers of trail dust," little realizing how prophetic his words would prove to be.

With only one barber and the bath house out back, the next door barbershop was convenient to the two mountain men. When they entered, the barber dropped his head to peer over his half-round spectacles at the two buckskin clad specimen that entered his shop. Before he could express his opinion, Scratch said, "Yes, we both want a bath and shave and haircut! So, who do ya wanna start on first? And where's your bath place?" The barber simply pointed to Jeremiah, then to the chair. With a nod of his head to the rear of the shop, he motioned Scratch to go that direction. Then shaking out the cape, he waited for Jeremiah to take a seat.

The two men that exited the barbershop did not resemble those that entered with the exception of the parfleche pouches they carried. Both were attired in dark trousers with linen pullover shirts and were well groomed. Jeremiah sported a goatee and mustache and sideburns to the bottom of his ears, while Scratch still had a full beard although it was trimmed short and was without a mustache. They returned their packages to the room then went to the dining room to eat what would be Jeremiah's first experience in an inn. Scratch, with his youth in the city was not a stranger to proper manners and courtesies and surprised Jeremiah when he ordered the meal. "We'll both have the beefsteak with potatoes and vegetables, coffee to drink, and don't overcook those steaks. Thank you," he ordered and turned away from the matronly looking woman that took his order. He smiled at Jeremiah, who sat with his mouth open, a wrinkled brow, and a questioning look in his eyes.

"Now that we're in the city, and needing to take on the air of prosperity, I find it proper to drop the mountain man slang and pretend to have a little dignity and refinement," he replied to the unvoiced question.

Jeremiah slowly reached up and tugged on the whiskers on Scratch's face, then said, "Whoaa, I just had to make sure it was you. The voice is the same, but ain't nuthin' else the same. I was just gettin' over the shock of what I looked like in the mirror back there, and now you ain't who you used to be. Does that mean I need to change a bit too?"

"If we talk like we should and act the part as well, then I think the rest of this whole shebang will go a lot better. We don't need any problems of our own doing, because there will be enough challenges to overcome as it is. So, this will be good practice for us, don't you think?"

With their meals set before them, Jeremiah let his eyes wander over the abundance that was in front of him. Starting to attack the meal, Scratch stopped him with a cough. Looking up to his mentor, Jeremiah watched as Scratch took knife and fork in hand and demonstrated to the inexperienced diner the proper handling of the table cutlery. Scratch's lesson in manners and propriety brought the image of the past with his family before him. At the head of the table was his father, to his right his mother, and to his left his sister. Jeremiah could see all of them before him while his mind's eye traveled over the room and the table and filled him with so many memories. Again a boy, he was asking his Mom why he had to have his school lessons done and why he couldn't spend the time hunting squirrels and rabbits, only to hear her response that he must be prepared for life when he grows up. If he could change the past, he would happily do his lessons without argument.

"Aren't you hungry?" The question from Scratch brought Jeremiah back to the table in the Inn, to which he responded, "Yes, yes I am. I was just reminded of lessons from long ago and when my Mother tried to teach me table manners."

The men shortly retired to their room in anticipation of their first night's sleep under a roof in several years. After sitting on the bed to remove his uncomfortable shoes and take off his trousers, Jeremiah felt the bed, and looked at the floor. Without a word, he threw a blanket on the floor with a pillow and turned to find Scratch had already done the same thing on his side. Both men chuckled at the other, then turned in for the night.

To Keep a Promise

Chapter Twenty-Four: Direction

EXITING THE SECOND STREET INN were two men that were attired as well as any of the prosperous business men in the community. Dark trousers, a white linen pullover shirt topped with a dark cravat and a brocade waistcoat, covered with a wool frock coat, Jeremiah stepped to the walkway and turned to look at his companion. Lucas, formerly known as Scratch, also wore dark trousers and a linen pullover shirt. However, he chose a loose fitting scarf at his collar and a plain waistcoat but he also had a woolen frock coat. Both men chose to do without hats. So they wouldn't feel completely out of sorts, Jeremiah had his Bowie knife in its scabbard on his left hip and his Colt Paterson revolver tucked in his waist at the small of his back, while Lucas had both his knife and flintlock pistol in his waistband slightly offset at each hip.

The woman in the dining room had given directions to the First African Baptist Church. In their discussion with her, Lucas had learned the church had moved to the old Methodist Meeting House on the corner, which was a short distance from their old clapboard building that was never in very good repair. With the growth of the church it was necessary to move and the location of the Methodist building made it convenient to its many members. A small hand lettered sign near the corner of the building directed the men to the pastor's study at the rear entrance of the church. As they entered the building, Jeremiah stepped in first with Scratch or Lucas close behind. The door to the pastor's study was open and the cluttered desk did little to hide the frosted curly head behind the stacked books. "Pastor Ferrill?" inquired Jeremiah. The man stood to his full height which brought him eye to eye with Jeremiah, both men standing just over six feet tall. With an extended hand, the pastor replied, "That's what I answer to, most of the time," as a welcoming smile spread across his clean shaven face. He was a big man but his friendly manner showed a kind face that eliminated any intimidation.

Taking his hand, Jeremiah said, "You're familiar with the story of the prodigal son, aren't you?" and turned to reveal Lucas. His frown showed a question, but was soon softened to a smile that poked dimples in his cheeks and stretched his arms wide to wrap Lucas in an overwhelming bear hug as he mumbled, "Lucas, Lucas, Lucas, my boy. I never thought I would see you again. Praise God, it's good to have you back!" He pushed him to arm's length to get a good look at his own prodigal, as his chest bounced in deep laughter of joy. "Praise the Lord, yessir, Praise the Lord! Sit down, sit down and tell me all about yourself and what you've been doing for these many years. And who's your friend here?"

The first few hours together were spent reminiscing and catching up on all the happenings with family and friends. Lucas learned both his natural mother and his adopted mother, Pastor Ferrill's wife, had died in the cholera epidemic of 1833. Scratch had been close to his adopted mother and he felt the arrow of sadness and regret pierce his heart, but learning that his father had been one of the few to stay in the city and serve the suffering victims filled him with pride. As his father shared the report of the growth of the church and impact his church was having on the issue of slavery, it led the conversation to the purpose of their visit. As Lucas shared the details, Pastor

Ferrill often glanced to Jeremiah and nodded his head in approval of the quest. Jeremiah interjected, "So, Pastor, we really need some help in where to start, how to go about it, and well, I guess just about everything," revealing an eagerness in his tone. Jeremiah still struggled with himself as to who and what he really was, the image he saw in the mirror just yesterday revealed an imposing figure of a man, but his thoughts now reverted back to his youth and the time with Ezekiel. Many times on this journey he allowed himself to dwell on soul searching and trying to identify who he was; the woodsman raised by Indians and Ezekiel, the white man with roots in Michigan territory, or the emancipator of slaves. It seemed that argument was coming to fruition now before Lucas' father and the pastor of this church.

"Tell me what you know about Ezekiel's family," directed Pastor Ferrill.

As Jeremiah related his recollection from the many talks with Ezekiel about Momma Sarah, his sister Elizabeth, and his brother Zach, a smile began to spread across the pastor's face. "Momma Sarah, as you call her, and her daughter Elizabeth are members of my church. I see them every Sunday right here! Why, they've been members longer than I've been here!" he exclaimed. "But I don't recall them ever speaking of a son or brother. Course, that doesn't mean a lot, because it's not unusual for families to be split up when one or more are sold. Why, I've even had to change the wedding vows to, 'until death or distance do you part.'"

"Well Scratch, I mean Lucas," he said with a grin, "has already told you what we want to do, so, do you know where we can find them?" inquired Jeremiah.

"Yes, but, we need to think about this a bit. Let's go over to the parsonage and we'll have a bite to eat and see if we can't put a little substance to this idea of yours," directed the pastor. As they sat around the table in the kitchen of the parsonage, the three men became very intent in their discussion. The pastor was thorough in his considerations of all possible questions and scenarios that might be presented before them. He assured the men of the necessity of a proper background and plan to present to any prospective inquiries, a plan that included the proposed property for the farm or plantation, the need for what type of slaves or workers, the timetable required for the purchase and preparations, and any other purchases of equipment or supplies to provide credibility to their story, and of course, the plan for afterwards and the future.

By the time the trio had exhausted all the possibilities and nuances of the proposed action, they agreed it was time to put on the feed bag. Since the pastor now lived alone in the home, Lucas pitched in as they prepared somewhat of a meal from his previous nights leftovers. All Jeremiah was interested in was the fresh pot of coffee on the side plate of the Majestic wood burner kitchen stove. Grabbing one of the tin cups hanging from a hook beside the window, he poured himself a cup of the dark brew and with a motion of the cup offered to do the same for the other men. As they returned to the table, the pastor stretched his hands to each side to grasp the hands of both Jeremiah and Lucas, then bowed his head and began to pray. "Our most precious God and Father, we come to you now as your humble servants with our hearts heavy with the need of freedom for our brothers and sisters. We ask you God to direct our thoughts and our steps as we seek to go forth and accomplish your work. Jeremiah and Lucas have an awesome task set before them and they can only do this with the power of Almighty Heaven surrounding them and our Blessed Savior walking with them. Father, we ask that your Holy Spirit will prepare the way and the hearts of those involved and go before them. Blind the eyes and hinder the way of those that would prevent them, and show them the way to go to freedom. Lord, we commit our way to you and trust you. Through the power of the shed blood of Jesus and in His precious name we pray. Amen and amen."

Jeremiah was almost afraid to open his eyes and lift his head, but as the pastor released his hand, he slowly raised his head and reached for his cup. He had never experienced prayer like this, when someone talked to God like He was in the room with him. This personal contact was different than what he knew in his family home but somewhat like what he had known with Ezekiel. When Ezekiel prayed, it was as if there was no one else around and only he and God could hear what was being said, but with Pastor Ferrill, it was as if he was not only talking to God personally, but to everyone else within earshot, as if he was reaching out and wrapping everyone in his big arms for a blessed hug.

Henry Clay was a prominent figure in Kentucky, a well know lawyer and plantation owner, he had served in the United States Senate and House of Representatives and also as Secretary of State. He had recently returned from Washington and a failed campaign for president. Although a slaveholder, he was known to be kind to his slaves and Pastor Ferrill knew of his sympathies for freedom for his slaves. It was because of this knowledge that Pastor Ferrill thought Mr. Clay might be willing to part with some of his slaves, and since Momma Sarah was one of his long-held slaves, he knew it would take some convincing to accomplish Jeremiah's task. The Clay estate, known as Ashland, was a short distance from downtown and the buggy carrying Jeremiah and Lucas soon pulled in front of the palatial home. Stepping down from the buggy, Jeremiah led the way up the expansive steps to the large double door entrance and used the brass knocker to announce their presence.

The door opened to reveal a tall black man attired in black trousers, a white linen blouse with string tie under a black waistcoat. He had a sprinkling of white in his well groomed hair and the wrinkles in his face and neck revealed his age. Looking at the visitors, he said, "Yessuh, kin I hep you suh?"

Jeremiah nodded his head slightly and replied, "Is Mr. Clay available, we have a little business we would like to discuss with him?"

Stepping back and opening the door to reveal a large foyer with marble tiled floor and a large two tiered stairway illumined by a towering leaded window, he said, "Step in, suh, and I'll ask if Mr. Clay can see you."

The heels of his boots clicking on the marble tile announced the arrival of the distinguished man attired in a gold brocade waistcoat over dark trousers and a wide turnover collared shirt held close to the throat with a dark cravat. His high forehead held the slightly disheveled receding shock of white hair that tumbled over his ears and framed a mature slender face with bright friendly eyes. He extended his hand with long slender fingers and looked at his visitors with a question, then stated, "Gentlemen, I am Henry Clay. To what do I owe the pleasure of your company?"

"Mr. Clay, I am Jeremiah Thompsett, and this is my overseer, Lucas Ferrill. We have been referred to you as we are in need of both counsel and assistance."

"Interesting, interesting, well, let's go into the parlor and have a seat where we might discuss your pressing needs." With a slight bow and a wave of his hand to direct the men to the proper room, he stepped back and allowed them to enter the parlor, as he carefully watched and evaluated his visitors. A grouping of four upholstered chairs were gathered around a square table near the large floor to ceiling windows and at the direction of their host, Jeremiah and Lucas pulled chairs out from the table and seated themselves as Mr. Clay stood opposite. "I'm going to have a cup of coffee, would either of you gentlemen care for a cup?" Both Jeremiah and Lucas nodded their head in the affirmative then turned to take in the view provided by the large windows. When their host seated himself, he looked to Jeremiah and raised his eyebrows in a question and an invitation to begin.

"Mr. Clay, I have a claim filed on some property that has been vacated by the Chickasaw Indians. It lies South of Bardstown and straddles the Green River. It has some very fertile soil and shows a lot of promise. I intend to establish a farm there and I need a little advice on types of crops you might recommend to start with, and I will also need some workers. I was speaking with Pastor Ferrill in town and he recommended you on both counts," shared Jeremiah.

"Pastor Ferrill, hum, he's a good man. He's done a lot for this community. So, I'm a little familiar with the area you're talking about. Since you're just starting out, I wouldn't recommend anything but tobacco. It takes a little while to get it established, but the demand for it is increasing and I believe if you start out with it, it will pay off handsomely for you. Do you know anything about farming tobacco?" he asked with a hopeful look to Jeremiah and then to Lucas.

"No sir, I came from the South and my only experience is with some cotton and mostly with grains, like oats and wheat," replied Lucas.

Jeremiah spoke up, "Well, that's the other need. I was thinking that you might have an experienced field hand or two that would know their way around the crops, and you might be willing to part with some. Also, we will need a cook and helper around the house, because neither Lucas nor myself do very well in a kitchen," he said with a chuckle.

"Well, I do have some that would be able to do all you ask, and this is the right time of year to be in the buyer's market, but I'm not real sure about all that. I have had most of my negras a long time and I wouldn't want any of them mistreated. I have been thinking that I have too many and it might be good to let some of them go. Do you have much experience handling slaves?" he asked, directing his question at both men.

"Some, but I know this, they are people and people of any color respond to however they are treated according to the way they are treated or respected. I've spent time around both Indians and negras and have learned to see past colors and cultures'" replied Jeremiah earnestly. The unusual comments caused the elder statesman to look at Jeremiah with a penetrating gaze that caused the younger man to drop his eyes to his coffee cup. As Mr. Clay continued his examining stare, it became evident the man was not only considering the sincerity and character of the young farmer-to-be, but also measuring his own heart and motives. He turned his gaze to the windows and his expressionless face appeared as a sculpted bust more suited to a distant gallery of greatness. He had a stately manner about him that was a testament to his history of service to his community and state, but also to his commitment to family and what he considered to be an extended family that included all his workers. For some time he had wrestled with the virtue of slavery, and had many in-depth discussions with his fellow legislators concerning the viability of the continuation of the issue.

"Maybe it would be best if we discuss this with some of the workers, and maybe some answers will present themselves. Let me fetch a coat, and we'll go to the quarters and visit a bit on the way," he said as he stood and turned to the doorway. Jeremiah and Lucas rose to follow him to the foyer where Mr. Clay summoned his butler to secure a coat. As he slipped on the greatcoat, he said, "Since we're getting close to the evening meal, most of the workers will either be there or will soon be. So, how soon do you want to go to your property?"

"Actually, we are quite anxious to get started. We'll need to pick up some supplies in town, a few tools and such, and if we accomplish what we need here, we could leave as early as the morrow," replied Jeremiah. This prompted Mr. Clay to hesitate a step and turn to the men, "Well, you are anxious. What do you hope to get accomplished at this time of year? You can't plow any fields and it's certainly too early to plant."

"No, you're right about that, but we need to get started on housing for both the workers and for me and Lucas here. It shouldn't take too long to put up a couple of cabins and we'll use some of miner's tents for temporary shelter. That's one of the many reasons we'll need a couple of good workers to help us and of course a cook and maybe a helper for the most necessary item, our food," explained Jeremiah. The answer seemed to satisfy the older man. As they stepped into the door at the end of the long two story clapboard quarters building, they obviously were in the kitchen. Several women were busily preparing the meal for all the workers, counting the kitchen help there were twenty-six in all. Three women, one older and two probably in their late 30's, worked without acknowledging the visitors. The older woman was peeling potatoes with a practiced hand, dropping the peelings into a bucket and the skinned potatoes into a large pot half-filled with water. A casual look from her dark eyes revealed nothing but boredom and disinterest.

"Since there's just a few of you, Sarah there might be able to do the job. We've got two younger ones that have taken over more of the work here in the kitchen. But she's a good cook, been with me a long time." At the name Sarah, Jeremiah looked at the woman who now stared back with a surprised look revealed by the whites of her eyes. All slaves knew they were subject to sale at any time, but just like anyone else, after being in one place for a long time, they thought of it as home. The idea of leaving home was especially difficult for an older person, and Sarah was starting to show her age with the once coal black hair now more white and gray. Her wrinkles told the story of many hard years, but her eyes were still bright, especially now that a possible move loomed.

With his back to the woman, Jeremiah turned to Mr. Clay and asked, "I believe that whenever slaves have family, it's best to keep family together. It makes it easier to work when they're not worried about absent family members. Wouldn't you agree, sir?" he asked as he looked to the plantation owner.

"I believe you're right, Mr. Thompsett. And I appreciate your consideration in that manner. I believe the only family that Sarah has left is a daughter, Elizabeth. She also works here in the kitchen but sometimes her duties require her to do occasional cleaning in the quarters."

Turning to Sarah, Jeremiah asked, "So Sarah, did you not bear any sons? A sturdy woman like yourself?" To which she responded, "Yessuh, I bore two fine sons. But they's both gone to be wit da Lawd. One run away many years back, and the youngest, he died wit da cholera." The weight of the loss remembered caused her to drop her head and her gaze lingered on her now idle hands.

"Well, an experienced mother like yourself, surely you've brought others under your wing of protection?" inquired Jeremiah.

"Yessuh, there be two younguns that was friends of my Zachariah. I kinda 'dopted dem. That be Matthew and Marcus, good boys, bof of 'em," smiled Sarah, as she thought of the two young field hands.

"The Matthew she speaks of is one of the field hands that I thought might have the experience with tobacco that you need. He and Marcus are brothers and they've been with me for several years now. Haven't had much trouble with either of them," commented the statesman.

After spending time to meet the other workers, question Matthew about the crops, and touring some of the fields of the plantation, the three men returned to the main house and resumed their conversation at the table. Jeremiah and Lucas had visited on the return walk and now spoke regarding the workers. Lucas said, "Well, Mr. Thompsett, I think those two brothers, Matthew and Marcus would do for now, and we can look for others as the work requires. As far as the kitchen or house help, I don't know anything about that so whatever you decide is fine with me."

Turning to Mr. Clay, Jeremiah said, "I agree with Lucas, and I think the older woman Sarah and her daughter would do fine for the household work, cooking and all. Would you be willing to let the four of them go?"

"Well, first we would, of course, have to agree on the price. And second, I would want your word as a gentleman that they would be treated properly and with kindness," he responded.

"I will definitely give you my word that they will be treated as well if not better than they have ever been treated. Now as to the price, here's what I propose; $400 for the old woman,

$600 for her daughter, and $800 each for the two brothers," offered Jeremiah. Pastor Ferrill had given him a quick education on the going price of slaves and Jeremiah wanted the offer to be fair and not easily rejected. Henry Clay sat back in his chair without losing the direct eye contact with Jeremiah, and his expression betrayed his surprise at the offer. He knew it was fair, but he could not give in too easily as the unwritten rules of bartering and dickering required some give and take.

"$2600 is a good offer, but an even $3000 would be even better," he returned.

"Mr. Clay, you already know we are anxious to get started, so if you will draw up the papers, have the four ready to leave in the morning, I will deliver into your hands a total of $2800 cash when we return," countered Jeremiah.

Henry Clay extended his hand to seal the deal, and smiled broadly as they shook hands.

To Keep a Promise

Chapter Twenty-Five: Emancipation

LUCAS SLAPPED THE HIPS of the horse with the reins to start the buggy back to town, he was a high stepping black gelding that enjoyed strutting in front of the buggy and making the staccato rhythm on the cobblestones of the main street. There was much to do and the two men divided the duties to facilitate their soon departure. Before leaving the livery, Jeremiah spoke with the livery owner and blacksmith, Sam, regarding the purchase of a wagon and team for their journey. As Sam unharnessed the black from the buggy, he said, "I've got just the thing fer ya. Had a farmer go belly up last week and I bought the wagon so he could take his wife and go back where he came from. He said he weren't cut out fer farmin' nohow. I'll make ya a deal on it and the team and harness. It's right out back, go take a looksee." While Jeremiah negotiated with Sam, Lucas went to the parsonage of Pastor Ferrill to ask the Pastor to prepare the papers for manumission for the four slaves. After making the deal with Sam, Jeremiah went to the room at the Second Street Inn to await Lucas before going to the dining room for their dinner.

After breakfast in the dining room, the men carried their gear to the livery to pick up the wagon. Stowing the gear in the tack room with the rest of the packs and tack, both men mounted the wagon for the short trip to the plantation of Henry Clay. A quick stop at the general mercantile enabled Jeremiah to drop off the list of supplies they needed as he assured the clerk they would return yet that same morning to pick up the requested items. As Jeremiah rode beside Lucas his mind was busy carefully examining all the details of the undertaken task. There was still much to do before it would be done, but it felt good to be involved in the heart of the matter instead of just traveling to the distant destination, a destination that often seemed too far and too uncertain to ever reach. Yet, here they were, on the way to pick up the last of Ezekiel's family. If only Ezekiel were here to relish this moment.

Although it was still the early part of the morning, when they arrived at Ashland manor the four negras were standing together at the side of the large home. While Jeremiah mounted the steps to the door, Lucas went to the slaves to direct them to the wagon. Jeremiah was ushered into the home and directly to the parlor where Henry sat at the table with papers before him. He stood as Jeremiah entered the room, extended his hand and offered a chair at the table. "These are the papers for all four as agreed. I've signed them over to you and I'm sure you'll find them in order," he stated.

Jeremiah withdrew a heavy draw-string leather pouch from his waistband and sat it on the table before Henry Clay. "Likewise, as agreed," he stated simply, as he pulled the papers before him. While Jeremiah gave the papers a cursory examination, Henry Clay hefted the pouch and asked, "Gold coin? My, I certainly didn't expect that. I thought maybe a bank draft or paper currency, but I am very pleased to receive the coin. Yessir." The two men rose and exited the front door of the grand home to join Lucas by the wagon. All four of the slaves were seated in the bed of the wagon and each clasped their respective bags of belongings. The two field hands looked at Henry Clay in askance but received only a nod from the wrinkled face with the receding crown of white unruly hair.

194

Turning to the matriarch of the quartet, Mr. Clay said to Sarah, "I'm saddened to see you go, Sarah, but I believe you going with this young man will be the best for your future. I have confidence in him and he assured me that all of you will be well taken care of and treated very well. So, I'm trusting you all will make me proud and do a fine job for him," and with the briefest of goodbyes, he turned back to mount the stairs to his home.

Lucas and Jeremiah stepped from the front wheel hub to the spring mounted seat of the wagon, picked up the reins and slapped the team into action. The short trip back into town was without any conversation but was accompanied by the squeak of the wheels and rattle of the trace chains. As the wagon pulled to a stop in front of the general mercantile, Jeremiah told Lucas to get the horses and tack from the livery and meet on the road leaving town. With a nod of his head, Lucas started the short walk; he would pass by the parsonage and pick up the papers from Pastor Ferrill. Jeremiah was aware of the need of his friend to have some time with his adopted father and to say his goodbye, perhaps his last goodbye to his father.

"Matthew, Mark, give me a hand with these supplies," stated Jeremiah as he stepped to the boardwalk and turned to enter the mercantile. As he settled up with the clerk, the two field hands started carrying the supplies to the wagon. Jeremiah picked up the last parcel and turned to return to the wagon when he heard a loud ruckus just outside the door. When he stepped through the door, he spotted two men, obviously drunk, harassing the two field hands. The larger of the two would-be bullies had pushed Marcus back against the side of the wagon causing him to drop his parcels, while the dirtier one was cursing at Matthew. Jeremiah spoke quickly and firmly to the two drunks, "Get your hands off those men!" Hearing the warning, the larger man turned away from Marcus and leaned back against the wagon to steady himself, and with slurred words said, "And what nigger lover is gonna stop me?"

Jeremiah dropped his eyes from the man, made a slight turn as if he was returning to the store, and with the speed of a striking snake, he spun back in a slight crouch and let fly the Bowie knife. The blade buried itself two inches in the wooden side of the wagon and parted the legs of the assailant. The top edge of a Bowie knife has the foremost 5 inches as sharp as the bottom cutting edge, and that edge had split the crotch of the drunkards trousers and threatened to do even more damage. The drunk had risen to his tip-toes and froze in place as he stared at the pending difference in his singing bass or soprano. As he slowly lifted his head he found Jeremiah standing between him and his partner, holding the Colt Paterson revolver aimed at his head. With a calm and low voice, Jeremiah said, "Now, would you men like to apologize to my workers and maybe I'll let you go on your way?"

"I ain't 'pologizin' to no nigger!" shouted the smaller of the two. At the click of the hammer cocking on the revolver, the knife-suspended man said, "Dammit, Spade, do what he says!"

With apologies made and supplies loaded, Jeremiah mounted the wagon and started the trip out of town. Within a few miles, Lucas joined them as they pulled to the side of the road. Jeremiah stepped down from the wagon, went to his horse and dug in the parfleche and with a nod to his partner, grabbed his buckskins and stepped beside his horse to get back into his comfortable attire. Both men grinned at the newfound comfort and security of their attire, horses, rifles, and rural surroundings. Jeremiah looked up at Lucas who was still seated atop his black gelding and asked, "So, can we drop this Lucas stuff, it just don't suit you Scratch?"

"Wal, I hope ta shout. I'm tired of everthin' 'bout the city and them slicked up phonies that think they're so all-fired special."

As Jeremiah stepped in the stirrup of his saddle and swung his leg over, with a nod of his head he directed Matthew to drive the wagon and follow along. With the wagon, it was necessary to forego the previously covered hillside trail and travel the road as it made its way through the valley below the mountain ridge. Their destination was Owensborough and that would take about four days of riding. Though traveling the roads, both men preferred to make camp in the trees and away from the other travelers. Occasionally Jeremiah would drop back and check on the wagon's occupants and the condition of the equipment. During one such survey, he noticed Marcus and Elizabeth were often in deep conversation and usually quite close together. As he spurred his horse forward, a slight smile tugged at the corner of his mouth as he was thinking about the response each would have when, after they made camp for the night, he revealed the plan for their future. As dusk approached, Scratch noticed a small stream that dropped from the ridge and merged with the creek in the bottom of the valley. A sizable grove of trees sheltered a clearing next to the stream and offered a good campsite. Scratch motioned to Jeremiah and both men left the roadway to prepare the campsite, before he stepped down from his Dapple grey mount, Jeremiah waved to Matthew to bring the wagon. As they pulled to the clearing, Jeremiah said, "Matthew, you and Marcus gather us some firewood and start the fire. Sarah, if you and Elizabeth would work on our supper I think we'd all appreciate it. There's a coffee pot and a fryin' pan in our packs here, but anything else you need should be with the supplies we got at the mercantile." Jeremiah and Scratch unsaddled their horses, relieved the pack horse of his panniers and packsaddle and hobbled the three. The team at the wagon was stripped of the harness and led to the grassy knoll with the other horses. Scratch and Jeremiah busied themselves with rearranging the packs, parfleches, and panniers as well as the supplies stacked in the wooden crates in the wagon. Supper was soon ready and the ladies summoned the men to join them.

After the meal was finished and the clean-up done, the group casually gathered around the campfire with each staring into the flames and immersing themselves in thoughts of both past and future. The uneasy silence was soon broken by

Jeremiah as he said, "Well folks. I think its time for me to share a few things with you. You see, it wasn't just happenstance that we ended up going to Henry Clay's plantation in search of just any slaves. It all started with you, Momma Sarah."

The surprise on her face brought wide open eyes that searched Jeremiah for an answer as she quickly responded, "Me? Why me?"

"Well, actually it started quite a long time ago," shared Jeremiah. As he began the story that started with his first meeting Ezekiel, the attention of each one was glued on the words and facial expressions of the storyteller. As the story progressed, tears often filled the eyes of both Momma Sarah and Elizabeth as they thought of the son and brother of so long ago. There was laughter, sobs, gasps and many other responses from the quartet of listeners but each one seemed to move a little closer and grow more and more interested in the special tale told by this almost stranger. "And so, this all amounted to a promise made to the man that was the greatest influence in my life. A promise that had to be kept, no matter the cost in time, effort, and expense. So, now, Scratch has something for each of you," he shared as he nodded to Scratch to give each of them the papers of manumission.

The confused looks on the faces of the four quickly revealed their inability to understand the papers before them. Although Elizabeth could read a little, the legal papers were beyond her comprehension. Scratch then spoke, "What those papers say is, you are free! You are no longer slaves and you can do whatever and wherever you darn well please. Ya don't have ta answer to nobody!" They collectively looked up at Scratch then swiveled their gaze to Jeremiah as one. The whites of their eyes betrayed their surprise and disbelief and confusion. Momma Sarah was the first to speak, "Ya mean it? Is this real? We be free?" As both Scratch and Jeremiah nodded and smiled, the other three former slaves began to shout and jumped up to dance around the fire.

After the initial excitement, the winded celebrants collapsed to their places on the log and rocks by the fire. The broad smiles revealed the depth of joy and thankfulness that now dwelt in each heart. As they regained some composure, Momma Sarah, said, "Oh my, praise da Lawd, praise da Lawd. Mr. Jeremiah and Mr. Scratch, thank you. Thank you so much. We cain't even begin ta thank you 'nuff," she said with tears again tracking down her cheeks. "But, what we gonna do now? Where we gonna go?"

"Momma Sarah, the one that made it all possible is your son, Ezekiel. It was his burden and goal in life to see you free. Now, as to what to do, we'll talk about that in the next few days. We've got things lined out for you and you don't need to worry about it none. Of course, it will all be up to you, but I think you'll like what we have in mind," replied Jeremiah.

To Keep a Promise

Chapter Twenty-Six: Freedom

THE SMALL CARAVAN topped the slight knoll that
overlooked the settlement of Owensborough, a familiar sight
to both Jeremiah and Scratch. The yellow banks on the
opposite side of the river rose as a frame for the small
community and its scattered buildings. With only one brick
building of any size, the remainder of structures appeared as
copies of one another with the clapboard siding and false fronts
on the few businesses that lined the main street. Scratch
suggested, "Why don't we camp in that same spot and maybe
we'll find Thaddeus again," he stated with a wave of his arm to
the West of town. It wasn't that long ago that the two travelers
had grounded their canoe and made camp on their first arrival
to the banks of the Ohio. The clearing was empty and the
firepit was full of the charred remains of a previous campfire
as the wagon halted by the now leafless trees. After four days
of travel, the camp routine was established and each turned to
their respective duties.

"Hello the camp," came a shout from deep in the woods as
a rag-tag figure of a man began to emerge. He hesitated as he
saw the familiar faces of Scratch and Jeremiah and said, "What
happened? Did you fellas lose your way an' haf ta' come back

here? I spose ya need an ol' river rat ta' show ya the way again," he cajoled with a wide grin on his face.

"Lookee here, Jeremiah, looks like some big ol' catfish done spit up his dinner right here on this ol' sandbar. Guess there are some things even a catfish can't stomach," replied Scratch as he approached the river rat with his hands extended in welcome.

After supper was over and the campfire chatter resumed, Scratch walked out of the ring of light with his arm around the shoulders of Thaddeus. "Thaddeus, my friend, a mutual acquaintance of ours, Pastor Ferrill of Lexington, told me you were the man for a job we need doin'. As you see, we've got some friends here and we would shore like ta' git 'em 'cross the river an' on their way up North. Now, the Pastor, who happens to be my daddy, said you would know what station the train needs to go through and what conductor could take care of it, is that right?"

At the mention of Scratch's relationship with the pastor, Thaddeus pulled back to get a better look at Scratch, then said, "Your daddy?"

"Well, more like my adopted daddy, but he raised me anyhow," replied Scratch. "Now, whatcha say, kin ya do it?"

"Mebbe, but it'll take some doin' ya know, gotta git a boat an' all," he surmised.

"Well, we found our canoe right where we left it and it's fine, so tomorra we're gonna take these here horses and wagon to the livery and maybe we kin make a trade. Mebbe git ya bigger boat an' whatever else ya need. Think that'd work?" Scratch questioned.

While Scratch communed with Thaddeus, Jeremiah and the others sat around the campfire and talked about the suggested plans for their future. As the conversation lulled, Jeremiah turned to Momma Sarah and in a low voice told her, "Momma Sarah, Ezekiel left you with some money which I'll give you before you leave. It should be enough, that if you want to, you could maybe buy a little farm or some property and if you and the boys there work it, you would probably be able to live pretty well for the rest of your days. But remember, this is for you and your daughter as provided by Ezekiel."

"Well now, how did he git all this money? I know my boy wouldn't steal it, so how'd he git it?" she inquired.

"We did a little gold panning and mining up in the mountains, and we saved it up for this day," he said grinning. "All Ezekiel ever talked about was his Momma Sarah."

"Well, that's all well and good fer me, but what 'bout you?"

"Oh, there's more where that came from. Don't worry 'bout me," he assured her.

"No, I don' mean money. What 'bout you and da Lawd? Do you know da Lawd as yo' Savior? Are you sure 'bout Hebbin'?" she asked with deep pleading eyes.

The conversation that followed revealed the time in the past when Jeremiah had sat at the knee of Ezekiel as he read his Bible and told Jeremiah about the love of the Lord Jesus. It was then that Ezekiel led the young man in prayer to receive Christ as his Savior and to ensure a place in Heaven. As he shared the experience with the old woman, tears welled up in her eyes and then rolled down her cheeks as a smile painted her face with gladness. To know that her son was still close to the Lord in his final days gave her heart a special comfort and her life contentment.

After breakfast the following morning, Jeremiah, Thaddeus and Scratch took the horses and wagon into town to the Livery they bought the horses from just a couple of weeks before. With minimal negotiation an agreed upon price was paid, and although the Liveryman did not have a boat to trade, he referred them to another business man that might be able to accommodate them. A short walk up the street brought them to the office of a dentist and veterinarian with a sign hanging over the boardwalk in the shape of a tooth with the identifying words hand written over the top. With a short visit to the man, all four men went to the riverside below the town to view the boat for sale. Larger than a normal wooden fishing row boat, it was the type usually carried by larger ships to transport cargo to and from shore. Again, a brief period of negotiation led to the men becoming the new owners of a boat the dentist thought he would never sell, and all left happy with the deal made.

With their campsite downstream from town, it was easy for the three men to maneuver the craft and beach it alongside the now uncovered canoe. Jumping to the shore and securing the craft with a rope to a tree, Thaddeus asked the men, "Are these free men or escapin' slaves?"

"Free. They have their papers with them. But we thought it best for them to be able to start a free life, they go North to a non-slave state to establish their new home."

"That makes it easier then. We can load up and cross over in daylight. We can make connections when we git to th' other side easy 'nuff."

The divided supplies and gear were loaded into the boat while Jeremiah and Scratch took their now dwindled rations and packs to the birchbark canoe. As the wooden boat was untethered and pushed from the sandbar, the four free blacks and their guide prepared to board. As Sarah turned to Jeremiah, she said, "We can never thank you 'nuff, but know this, you will allus be in my prayers," and as her eyes began to well up with tears, she added, ". . .now come ober here and give Momma Sarah a hug." That began the round of hugs, handshakes and goodbyes that ended with a grunt and a mumble from the river rat as he began to push the boat towards the water.

"Come on now, we need tag it ta goin'" he ordered as the small group began to climb into the high side-walled boat. Thaddeus instructed Matthew to push them off as he reached for one of the oars and directed Marcus to the other. Putting his shoulder to the prow, Matthew dug his feet in the sand and pushed. With a couple of steps in the water, he jumped into the boat to take his place on the foremost board seat in the prow. The two oarsmen pulled deep in the water and the boat easily slid towards the current. Jeremiah and Scratch watched the progress of the water travelers until they disappeared downstream. They would travel about five miles downstream then would meet the Underground Railway conductor just East of Evansville, Indiana, and continue on their journey North and to their ultimate home in freedom.

Scratch turned to Jeremiah and said, "Wal, we better git goin' if we're gonna try to ketch one o' them paddlewheel riverboats goin' North ta St. Louie! It shore seems like a bit of a let-down after all th' excitement we been havin' but boy, you kin shore hold yore head high, cuz you done did what you said!"

"Yeah, sure makes ya feel good, tho, don't it? Knowin' they're gonna have a life that's free just like Ezekiel wanted."

"Well, free or not, I think that Marcus is gonna surrender his freedom purty soon."

"What do you mean?" asked Jeremiah.

"Didn't you see the way them two, Elizabeth and him, was makin' cow eyes at each other?"

As the two men finished settling the packs and paraphernalia in the canoe and made ready to leave, Jeremiah stepped to the middle of the clearing, lifted his head and hands upward and called out, "Ezekiel, it's done. I kept my promise. Your family is free!" Then dropping his head, he paused for a short while, then with long and purposeful strides to the canoe, he said to Scratch, "Let's go to the mountains. I've got another promise to keep. Laughing Waters is waiting for me!"

THE END

To Keep a Promise

A look at Star Dancer by B.N. Rundell

This is a story about a horse and a boy, but not just any horse: a wild mustang stallion and not just any boy, but a native American proud member of the Arapahoe nation on the Wind River reservation in Wild Wyoming. When these two wild hearts are knit together through unique circumstances and challenges, they become a championship team.

Chastised by his peers and often excluded because of his disability, Trey Standingelk is more comfortable enjoying the solitude of long rides in the mountain with just his horse, his dog and his lifelong friend and often companion, Skye.

The two companions find themselves as the captors and eventual trainers of a beautiful mustang stallion, but Trey's challenges lend an obstacle that must be faced. After learning about the opportunities in the realm of horse training and especially the competitive arena of Free-Style Reining, Trey and Star's world is rapidly expanded. The connection that develops between the horse, Star Dancer, and Trey goes far beyond man and beast, and becomes a heart to heart lifelong bond.

To Keep a Promise

About the Author

Born and raised in Colorado into a family of ranchers and cowboys, B.N. is the youngest of seven sons. Juggling bull riding, skiing, and high school, graduation was a launching pad for a hitch in the Army Paratroopers. After the army, he finished his college education in Springfield, MO, and together with his wife and growing family, entered the ministry as a Baptist preacher.

Together, B.N. and Dawn raised four girls that are now married and have made them proud grandparents. With many years as a successful pastor and educator, he retired from the ministry and followed in the footsteps of his entrepreneurial father and started a successful insurance agency, which is now in the hands of his trusted nephew. He has also been a successful audiobook narrator and has recorded many books for several award-winning authors. Now finally realizing his life-long dream, B.N. has turned his efforts to writing a variety of books, from children's picture books and young adult adventure books, to the historical fiction and western genres which are his first love.

Discover more great titles by B.N. Rundell and Wolfpack Publishing at:

http://wolfpackpublishing.com/b-n-rundell/

To Keep a Promise

Made in the USA
Monee, IL
28 October 2020

46257362R00125